Wide Spaces

SHELLY CRANE

Reference: Useless facts found in *Uncle John's Monumental Reader,* www.dbmproaudio.com/facts.html,and the world wide web
Cover design by Okay Creations
Editing services by Hollie Westring
Formatting by Indie-Vention

Printed in the USA

1 2 3 4 5 6 7 8 9 10

Paperback available, also in Kindle and E-book formats through Amazon, CreateSpace, Barnes & Noble, Apple, Sony, Kobo, and anywhere else eBooks are sold.

More information can be found at the author's website:

http://shellycrane.blogspot.com

ISBN-13: 978-1493505104

ISBN-10: 1493505106

For
my nieces
Reagan, Samantha, & Caroline.

*I hope you know that men like
Mason and like your uncle Axel
DO exist. You just have to wait
for him to find you.*

Useless Facts

1. Just like fingerprints, everyone's tongue print is different.

2. Every day, more money is printed for Monopoly than the U.S. treasury.

3. Only 24% of Americans do not have a tattoo.

4. Peanuts are one of the ingredients in dynamite.

5. In the course of an average lifetime you will, while sleeping, eat 70 assorted insects and 10 spiders.

6. Cherries will cause cancer cells to kill themselves.

7. A teaspoon of honey is the life's work of 12 bees.

8. Dolly Parton once anonymously entered a Dolly Parton look-alike contest…and lost to a drag queen.

9. Studies show that 70% of people who marry their best friend stay married their entire lifetime.

10. Diet Coke destroys tooth enamel as much as meth and crack cocaine.

11. To remain in love for a lifetime : listen actively to your partner, ask questions, give answers, appreciate, stay attractive, include your partner, give

him/her privacy, be honest and trustworthy, tell your mate what you need, accept his/her shortcomings as who they are, give respect in all things, never threaten to leave, say 'no' to adultery, and cultivate variety in your activities to keep things fresh. You can never say 'I love you' too many times and you should say it every day. Even though you've been together forever it seems, you should still continue to 'date' your mate and find new ways to fall in love with them every. Single. Day.

Useless Fact Number One

Just like fingerprints, everyone's tongue print is different.

Mason

It wasn't that I was scared, per se. It was that the man hated the guts in my belly, and Emma was his first daughter to get married, even though she was the youngest, and…well, the man hated my guts.

Emma knew something was up. I'd purposely left the ring out in a hidden-but-not-really-hidden kind of way. I knew she'd seen it. Like a switch that was flipped she was different just like that. But when a couple days ticked by and I hadn't proposed, I could also see her disappointment. I hated that, but I had to ask her father for "permission" and I used that word lightly. Whether or not he agreed, I'd be marrying his daughter. I just wanted to use this last olive branch to hopefully toss off any doubt or contempt he held for me.

His retirement party was today. Emma was being introduced to a million folks by her mom so I saw my opportunity and went for it. He must have known somehow or seen it on my face maybe, because he set his drink to the side, maintained eye contact with me my entire walk over, and excused himself from the group of people he was with.

He ticked his head to the side when I reached him and said, "Let's talk in my office." Seriously ominous words.

I sat down on his lush beige couch and he sat next to me. I figured I wouldn't beat around the bush or insult his intelligence with small talk. I pulled the ring from my pocket, opened the lid, and turned it for him to see.

He took it easily and looked at it for an excruciatingly long time. Then he closed the lid, twirling it in his fingers. "You know, when I first met you and I saw how much passion and commitment you had for my daughter, I was thrilled. And now, as I look at your passion and commitment for my daughter, but in a completely different way, I have to admit that I felt unease at first."

I nodded. "I know, sir."

"Don't call me sir," he chided and sighed with a small smile. "You called me Rhett before you dated my daughter. The rules haven't changed. "

"Yes, s…Rhett."

We chuckled a little awkwardly. "It's not that I don't like you, Mason, I just-"

"You think I can't provide for her," I stated.

"It's not that either. Emma is a big girl and I trust her judgment on things. It's just…she wakes up, she doesn't remember us at all or want a whole lot to do with us, and then she takes one look at you and for whatever reason, she is completely latched onto you. We just wanted her back and then she…just wanted you."

I swallowed that down. Dang, I thought they didn't like me because I was poor. "I mean, Isabella said…"

"She said things because she was angry and because she grew up poor herself. She was angry with you, Mason, because we wanted our daughter back. That's all." He opened the box again and looked at the ring, his face blank giving nothing away. "But we had her all along. She still feels like that little girl who used to grab my coattails when I'd come in from work and ask me to make paper planes with her with my depositions." He chuckled. "I wasn't ready to let her go after just getting her back, and I'm still not."

I felt all the breath leave me in a rush. I opened my mouth to speak, but he beat me to it. "But Emma fits…with you. This whole world is different for her, and the way she looked at things, like a fish out of water, made me ache for her. But she seems to fit with you, and that makes her fit all the way around."

He snapped the box closed and handed it to me slowly. "Even before, my daughter was a very happy girl. But there's a difference between happy because that's all you've known and being happy because you've learned to be grateful and that makes you *really happy*, now isn't there?"

I waited, but he said nothing. "Yeah, there is."

"You make her the grateful kind of happy, Mason. And she may not live here anymore, but I know you're not taking her from us. She'll always be my little girl," he stated and gave me a look to make sure I was listening.

"Of course. I'm not trying to take her away. My mom's here; I wouldn't leave anyway."

"We know." He pointed at the ring and smiled, just barely. "She's going to say yes. You know that."

I nodded. I did know that. "I do."

"Then you already know what I expect of you. She'll be yours just as Isabella is mine. I take care of my wife. I not only provide for her, because that's not the most important thing, but I love her today more than I loved her the first day. If I had my way, my daughter would spend some time relearning who she is." I almost interjected that she knew exactly who she was, but his speech continued. "But she tells me that she knows, and that she's ready to move on. I don't know if she'll ever get her memory back. Of course, I have hope for that, but I just don't know. Emma holds her own fate in her hands. If she wants to do this, I'm going to give you my blessing."

All that for a yes. I sighed so loudly he had to have heard me. "Thanks, Rhett. I promise you don't have to worry."

He stood, sighing. "I know. Mason, we know you. It just took us off guard is all. You helped us when we were so lost for what to do after Emma's accident. You stayed with us for months and helped us and Emma. You could have passed us off or just not cared because no one thought she was going to make it. But you always believed." He held out his hand. "You're already a son to us, Mason. Now it's official."

I took his firm grip and felt a million pounds lighter.

When we went back to the party, I wondered if Emma would be able to decipher the smile on my face. We came back to find her and her mom giggling loudly at something the mayor was saying. He was a boisterous man, a cigar hanging out of half of his mouth, and he was waving his arms wildly to go with the story he was telling.

Em and her mom looked so much alike like that. Rhett and I stood and watched them for a while. Em was

13

wearing a short yellow dress and little black high heels. Her hair was down. She looked amazing and happy. There was that word again.

When they caught us gawking, they smiled. Her mom leaned over and whispered something, causing Em's smile to grow. I may have even seen a blush.

Rhett walked over to Isabella and Emma came to me.

"What was that about?" She looked back at her dad. He had the saddest smile on his face. She glanced back to me, curious. "Did something happen? Everything OK?"

"Yeah," I replied and kissed her forehead. "All is well in the world."

And now, as the freezing air sucked me out of my warm memory of that day, it was colder than I could remember it ever being.

I looked down at my little Eskimo Emma and couldn't help but smirk at her as she tried to jam the carrot into the snowman's face. He was as tall as I was and she could barely reach.

"Are you freaking kidding me?" she asked him. I snickered behind her. She turned to glare at me playfully. "You are absolutely no help, Mr. Wright."

"I like watching you try." I slid my arms around her back.

"You like watching my backside," she countered with her own smirk.

"That's what I said."

She laughed, her arms reaching around my neck. "Oh, my. What am I going to do with you?"

"There's a list a mile long of things."

She shook her head. "Tease. Are you going to be this mean when I'm your wife?"

"Absolutely." She held up the carrot. "What?"

"Fix him. Poor guy's miserable without all his appendages."

I grinned and took it, moving to him, and she saw where I was headed. "Mason Wright, don't you dare!"

"What?" I said innocently and moved toward the snowman's bottom half. "You said he needed all his appendages?"

She laughed and hit my back. "Don't you dare!"

At the last second of giving the snowman a heavy dose of pride, I changed course and stuck it in the spot for the nose. "I don't know what you were thinking, but I'm appalled if it was something dirty. It *is* almost Christmas."

"You're such a scoundrel," she joked and hopped up on my back.

"Now you can cross number eighteen off your list— A snowman that resembles Philip Seymour Hoffman. Check."

She giggled hard. Her teeth chattered against my neck as she hung on. I reached up and touched her cheek. "You're freezing, baby."

"Yes, I am. It's freaking freezing, Mr. Bigglesworth."

I laughed as I started back toward the house. "Our movie marathons are doing you some justice."

"Anyone who can't appreciate a good Austin Powers movie just isn't sane."

I laughed some more as my boots crunched and drudged through the thick snow of the front yard. Christmas was just two days away. Our first Christmas together. The first Christmas that Emma could remember. The first Christmas our families would spend together. The last Christmas we'd have that Emma wasn't my wife.

I put her feet to the porch when we reached it and we shook off the snow. Colorado certainly had its fair share of snow, but the hard, awful stuff usually stuck to the mountains. This year, we had snow almost every day since Halloween. My beater barely functioned on these kinds of months. But I never wanted Emma to worry about breaking down or being cold since the beater usually didn't heat up until you reached your destination. So, I sold the beater and leased a new model Dodge Ram truck outfitted with the best snow tires. There was no way she was freezing her tush off or getting stuck somewhere in all the snow. The house was paid off, but I still had lots of bills from mom's medical stuff.

I had been marketing and getting jobs like crazy over the summer for my tattoo shop. It was time to take this up a notch if this was going to be my real-life business from now on. So, I put on my big boy pants, as Emma would say, and rented a small space up town. When business kicked into high gear, I hired someone to help. Jax pays me a booth rental fee every month and it makes it easier on me to know I'm getting that amount no matter what. It just so happened to cover the building rental every month, too.

It all seemed to be working out so well.

It even looked like we may be able to hire another guy because business was doing so well. The summer vacationers were very into getting a tattoo to remember their trip. Or regret them, either way. I thought it would slow up when winter hit, but it hadn't. There weren't really many tattoo shops around there and with the college being so close, it seemed I had cornered the market.

For the first time in a long time, I felt like I could breathe. I felt like I wasn't being smashed and pressed, draining me of any and everything. For the first time, I felt like my life wasn't a testament to my guilt and shame. It was a testament to how love finds you in the strangest places, and hope clings to us in the nooks and crannies we never think to look.

The gap between the man I used to be and the man I was now was a wide space that was filled with all the ways Emma had saved and changed me.

I pulled her inside with me, the warm air making her groan with delight. I peeled off her hat and then her gloves and boots. I looked up at her from where I was crouched on the floor. "Better?"

"It's not fair that we're both out there in the cold, but I'm the only one who almost freezes to death every time," she muttered.

"I've got thick, manly blood," I rebutted.

She shook her head at me, letting her coat fall from her arms and slinging it to hook on Mom's hall tree. I did the same and Emma wrapped her arms around my middle, nuzzling her ice-cold nose into my neck. Gah, she *was* freezing.

"Since when did the Arctic take up residence in Colorado?" she griped.

I rubbed her arms and back, warming her as best I could. She placed her hand on my chest next to her face. She stared at the ring on her finger with the small, private smile that was proudly reserved for me. The ring wasn't massive by any stretch, and she wasn't being vain in her gazing. She'd told me several times that she stared at it so it would be burned in her brain permanently and even if another coma claimed her, it wouldn't take the memory of me asking her to marry me away from her.

She was thriving in her college classes, her family was blossoming before our eyes as they got to know their new daughter and vice versa. We had a date set. Emma and I both wanted nothing more than to have a small ceremony as soon as possible, but her parents being...*her parents*...wanted the big send-off they'd always planned for their daughter. Emma felt like she owed it to them to do it.

I knew the day would come that she would forgive herself for being different, that she'd be able to feel like she was worthy of being loved by her parents. She wasn't taking someone else's life; she was taking back what was hers all along. It was a slow process, but it was happening—a cocoon setting the butterfly free when it's ready.

I rubbed my thumb over her ring and down the length of her finger. "I love you, Em," I whispered into her hair.

"I love you." She leaned back to look up at me. She licked her lips before biting and gnawing on them. What was coming next always made my blood rise. That was her body's way of letting me know that she wanted to be kissed. I didn't wait for her to ask. I leaned in, licking my own cold lips to moisten and warm them for her before I settled onto her mouth.

Gah, that mouth.

She kissed like her life depended on it. She never played coy or teased. When she kissed me, it was with purpose. When she accepted my kiss, it was with everything she had. She was wide open. Our kissing was meaningful and all encompassing.

I leaned her back a little, her eyelids fluttering. "Baby, you're freezing. Here."

I took my jacket from the hook and wrapped it around her. "Thanks," she said softly. She looked at my neck and I could tell she was stalling. "Can I stay the night with you?" she asked slowly.

I felt my brow dip. "What will your dad say?"

"We're getting married on New Years," she replied and put her hand around my neck. "He'll say I'm an adult and about to be a married woman and I don't have to have Daddy's permission anymore." She grinned.

"That's not exactly what I meant, Em."

She sighed. "I know, but you've already gotten the man's blessing. You've got to stop worrying so much."

"Yeah, and I don't want his blessing revoked."

"I'll text Mom, tell her I'm staying over, and I'll see them tomorrow. She knows it's freaking cold out there and snowing like a mini-blizzard every five minutes."

That familiar sensation of doubt crept up. "I just don't want them to regret—"

"They won't. They don't." She pulled me closer with that hand behind my neck. "They see how happy I am because of you."

I gulped and nodded, the wave that had been crashing over me, receding. I still fought the fact that I was nowhere near good enough for her, not even in the same ballpark. Changing years of thinking you're nothing but a bastard trying to make up for things…took some time.

I sighed. She was right. Both of her parents had warmed up to me a lot. The day of her father's retirement party when I asked him not if I could marry her, because I was going to anyway, but if he would give us his blessing because I knew how much it meant to Emma, he said he was really surprised that I had come to ask him for it. That day he gave me his blessing to propose, and ever since then, he was different. He didn't spend so much time trying to avoid me and began to speak to me how he used to when I was Emma's physical therapist.

Two days later I took Emma back to the hospice. She got to see all the nurses, especially Mrs. Betty, and I got razzed to no end about being a sweetheart for getting fired because of a girl. I took her back to the rehab room. She was facing away from me, leaning against the parallel bars. I could tell in her peripheral that she was far away as she remembered and relived her time there. When she smiled at some memory, I knew it was safe to go in full speed.

"Em." My voice had been so low it was unrecognizable. She noticed the tone in my voice, too, and goose bumps spread across her skin under my hand. She turned, just her head, to look at me.

She smiled sweetly. "Yeah?"

I moved in slowly, letting one arm slide across her back to settle on her opposite hip and the other moved up to hold her face as she faced me. I let my forehead rest against hers, looking into her wide eyes as she waited for whatever I was about to say. When they fluttered almost shut, I knew I couldn't wait another second. I didn't have any pretenses prepared, nor did I want to use any. I wasn't interested in foreplay in this situation, no buildup. I went all in.

"Em, marry me," I whispered against her soft, white cheek. I felt the quick breath she sucked in all the way to my bones. I stayed right there, letting my thumb swipe across her cheekbone over and over. "In this room right here was the first time I fell in love with you, and I fell a little bit more every day. And then you showed me how you adored my mother and I *adored you* for it. Now…I want you to be mine. Not only do you make me a better man, but you make me happy. Marry me."

She turned her face quickly, further into my palm, and slammed her mouth on mine, pushing up on her toes. I took that as a yes and we tangled ourselves in a fashion that wasn't proper for a rehab room—in public—but that wasn't important. When I tasted her tears in our kiss, I wasn't worried. I knew her tears were from happiness because I knew she loved me. She showed me a million times a day in a million ways and I never doubted that.

It was the biggest compliment, those tears.

We had stayed in that room for far too long kissing the sense out of each other. When I finally pried myself away, I pulled the ring I'd gotten her from my pocket. She smiled at it lovingly and up at me. "I love you so much."

You, she said. Not I love *it* so much. You. That right there was why she was amazing.

Back to the present and out of my memories, I looked down at my Emma. "You want to say *hi* to Mom while I warm up some potato soup?"

She nodded before kissing my chin and making her way into the den. She pulled my jacket tighter around her and sat on the couch, going through the normal spiel with Mom that we did every day. I watched her from the doorway.

I watched the way she loved my mom.

She pulled the blanket around my mom's lap closer and gave her the remote, asking her if she wanted some hot tea, took out the photo album and tried to ready my mother for the way I'd look when I brought the soup in to her.

I loved Emma with my very being, and I didn't deserve her, but by God, she was mine. And I wasn't giving her up for anything.

Useless Fact Number Two

Every day, more money is printed for Monopoly than the U.S. treasury.

Emma

I put the albums back on the shelf after Mason put his mom in bed for the night. I looked around the place and realized how hard Mason was trying to make it look nice. It was a cute little house. Small, but cute. It did need some work, but it was by no means unlivable. He had painted the outside and fixed the porch, ripping out all the bad wood and replacing it. He'd even wanted to paint in the living room, but knew his mom needed to have everything the way it was to not scare her every time she opened her eyes. She needed to be eased into the new truth every day. I knew he was doing it all for me, because he thought it was some great chore for me to go from living in that beast of a house my parents called home to moving in with him after the wedding.

But it wasn't.

I felt like a small-town girl with small-town needs in my heart. I was so ready for our life to begin together. He worked on the outside of the house and the yard on the weekends and said he'd been slacking on his duties for too long anyway. He'd gotten a new truck, the beater long gone. The shop was doing really well. I got that. I just hoped he knew that it wasn't a sacrifice for me. I loved his mom, I loved their little house that she built with love for her boys, and I loved the fact that Mason took care of her himself instead of sticking her into some facility. It kind of irked me that he didn't see how I lit up when I came to see them.

I knew that my living there was going to be different. His mom needed things to be as close to her old life as possible, her doctors said, otherwise she could freak out and hurt herself or have a mental breakdown if she looked around and her entire surroundings were different. If she went to a facility, they'd pump her with meds to keep her sedated so she'd be in a constant state of 'calm'. No. I didn't want that.

I let my eyes settle on the photos on the mantle. All different frames, yet all blended perfectly to fit together in the small space. One of Mason and Milo on skateboards together on the street—Mason so much taller and a little ahead of Milo. Another one of all of them at Christmas in front of a small tree, grins on all their faces as they held marshmallow topped hot chocolate. Milo was a completely different person than the boy I met.

Then the one on the end was Mason when he was about sixteen. He had an acoustic guitar in his lap as he strummed something, sitting on the picnic table out back. I picked up the picture to look closer and could see half a record sticking out from under his pant leg along with pages of tabs. It was an LP of The Wallflowers. I felt my smile spread. He was so adorable.

Warm hands reached around my middle and the even warmer lips followed on my neck. I sank back into him and placed the picture back gently. "Who's that nerd?" he joked.

I slapped his hand. "Shut up. That guy's adorable."

"Back when he thought he had it all figured out." I heard the way his tone changed, but when I turned to look up at him, he was smiling. "I made hot chocolate and the DVR is paused and ready."

"Ooh…what is it?"

"Well…" he smiled tenderly, "we've breezed through the *Austin Powers* movies, *The Breakfast Club* and the rest of the Brat Pack movies, *Ron Burgundy*, and anything involving Ben Stiller included but not limited to *Dodgeball*, so I figured we could do a chick flick this time."

"OK," I told him and looked over at the mugs on the side table. "Ooh, hot chocolate."

He laughed. "You don't even care what the movie is?"

I took a cautious sip. "I trust you." I licked the foam from my lip.

He watched me with that Mason smile that I remembered from the very beginning. "What?" I asked quietly.

"Gah, just…" He shook his head slowly, and looked at me as he said, "I love you being here."

I smiled—unable to do anything but—set my cup aside and took his hand, pulling him toward the couch with me. "I love being here."

"This is what it will be like," he started. He watched and waited, I guess to see if that idea thrilled me or not. "This is what it will be like after the wedding. You, me, movies, Mom, dinner, normalcy."

"I can't wait," I breathed.

"New Years isn't that far away," he countered.

"Not soon enough for me." I wrapped my arms around his back and looked up at him. "I'd marry you right this second. You have to know that."

He leaned closer. "You'd really be fine getting married without all the crazy things your mom has planned for us? I mean, she has doves, Emma. Doves."

I giggled. "Of course. I'm not going to remember most of those people anyway." He twisted his lips. "Not self-deprecating, just saying."

"But I want those things for you," he countered and seemed to gather steam. "You deserve all those things. You've earned it."

I smirked. "And I win a prize?"

"You get me." He smirked back.

I laughed. "That's what I wanted. What a coincidence."

He grinned, shaking his head, and leaned down into my space. His big, warm, loveable hands took my face between the palms. I closed my eyes and remembered what those hands felt like on my hips as he helped me learn to take steps and manage my weight.

He tilted my head to the side a little, his thumb rubbing across my lips. I opened my eyes to an adoring, but sizzling look that made my heart thump harder.

"I love how you're so trusting with me," he murmured and leaned in. His lips brushed my cheekbone as he said, "I used to hate it." He sighed, long and meaningful and sexy. "I used to think it was a bad thing to give me so much, but now, when you close your eyes and just hang on for the ride, for whatever I have planned for you?" He took my earlobe between his lips and I gripped him tighter. "That makes me absolutely burn up when you do that."

I smiled and shivered. "My eyes are closed right now, Mason," I lied.

"What do you want me to do?" he asked. The back of the couch hit my butt. I hadn't even realized we'd been moving. "What do you want to trust me with tonight?"

A sigh escaped forcefully, waving the white flag that I was a melted, scorched woman at those words.

"Anything," I whispered back.

He lifted me to sit on the back of the couch, but left his arm hooked around my middle to keep me upright. He lifted my chin just as his hips slid between my knees.

"Emma," he spoke against my lips. He brushed his lips against mine several times. He had to know how on fire I was and yet he took his time and inched closer with every sweep. He must have heard my huff of frustration because he chuckled huskily before settling on my mouth fully.

I opened to him immediately, sighing with relief when he took over completely and tortured me with his powerful tongue. He cupped my hips to bring us together, so I slung my arms around his neck to keep me there.

The clock ticking in the background was the only sound except our kissing.

"Em," he groaned and took a long pull from my mouth. "Em, you're making that whole running away to get married thing sound really appealing right now."

"Don't tempt me, Mason." I tugged a little on his hair in my fist.

He groaned and moved his hot, agonizing mouth to my neck. "Gah, why do you always smell so amazing?"

I sighed into his hair. "Mason."

I moved my hand under his shirt to trace the tattoos I couldn't see. It made me feel as though I knew his body, every curve and line, without even having to look. But when I moved my hand to his chest and encountered a bandage, I froze.

"What's this?" The pre-wife in me took over and the concern jumped out of me in commands to know his welfare. "What happened?" He bit his lip a little and then cursed with a guilty smile on his face. "What?"

He sighed and leaned his chest back just a smidge, enough for me to see, but still close enough for me to be connected with him. He lifted his long-sleeve thermal shirt over his head. I gasped at what I saw. He had plenty of tattoos covering his body, but this was a new one.

He had "Em" tattooed over his heart in a pretty, swirly writing and "189" under it. I wanted to run my fingers over it, but the clear bandage was there to let it heal because it was so new. "Mason," I sighed.

"The *Em*," he explained, "that part should be obvious. *189* is the number of days you were in my care, the number of days I moved and exercised your legs and arms, the number of days I knew I'd get to see you, the number of days I watched your closed eyelids, waiting and hoping that you'd wake up."

I didn't even realize the tears that I felt burning had spilled over until he wiped one away. He continued, knowing I was overwhelmed. "I was going to show you on Christmas."

I sniffed and looked at it without looking away. "You didn't do it yourself, did you?" I teased.

He chuckled softly. "I got Jax to do it."

I finally looked up and licked my lips. "Did he call you a big softy?"

"Among other things." He leaned forward and kissed my nose. "It was worth it."

"Well…now my Christmas gift for you just sucks."

He laughed and held my face gently between his palms. "Baby, I don't care what you get me. I'll be happy.

You could get me a blender as long as I get to spend Christmas with you."

I smiled a little, letting my palms settle on his sides under his shirt. "Of course I'm going to spend Christmas with you." I licked my lips again. "Thank you, Mason."

"You're welcome."

"No…" I pulled a move from his playbook and took his face in my hands. His cheeks were deliciously scruffy. He took my hand and kissed my palm before putting it back to his face. "I don't know if I ever said thank you for taking care of me."

He looked down and shook his head. "It was nothing—"

I moved his face back up. "I mean it. Thank you."

He watched me. "You're welcome, Em."

When his fingers went around my back and inched into the waistband of my jeans, I knew he was imagining my tattoo, just as I always did to his, the fever pitch was back on point. He leaned in so close I could almost feel him touching my lips. The pause was weighted and heavy, so reverent that I opened my eyes to see what his face would look like. He was in that awed state of disbelief that he seemed to be saturated in, usually when I was practically begging him to kiss me. Like right now.

I moved forward to capture his mouth, but he backed away a small inch to evade me.

"Mason," I complained.

He smiled. It was a cross between a sexy grin and a smile of just happiness and nothing more. I couldn't help but smile at him when he was in this mood. He thought he was grateful to have my love, but I was just as awed at the way he loved and cared for me. I bit into my lip and tilted my head a little. I took a deep breath and let my eyes flutter a little with the passion that was currently coursing through my veins.

It wasn't very hard to show him how he was affecting me.

"Text your mom," he commanded softly. "Let's go to bed."

My heart beat entirely for that statement. He chuckled and moved to let his nose touch mine, just a little. "Emma?" he tried to coax me from my stupor.

"OK," I supplied and did as he asked. When I was done, I tossed the phone onto the chair a few feet away. I looked back up at him and eased my arms around his neck. "Now what, Mr. Wright?"

He returned back to pressing against me and kissed my nose. "No classes for two weeks, right?"

I shook my head. "Nope. I'm yours for two whole weeks."

He smiled. "For now. Soon, you'll be mine forever."

"I already am." Admiration bathed him, but I wanted more than that. I pulled his neck down to me and kissed him, showing him how insane he made me. He pushed my belly a little. It was too late when I realized what he was doing. I laughed as my lips let go and I fell backward onto the couch cushions. I giggled even harder as he climbed effortlessly over the top to land on me gently. He pushed my knees apart with his big hand and settled onto me easily. I lifted my knee and put my heel on the back of his leg, so comfortable and happy with him.

I felt his warm fingers on the skin just under my shirt as he slanted his mouth over mine slowly. When I pushed both of my hands into his hair, he sighed, bathing my neck with warm, sweet breath. "So…I thought we could start moving some of your things in this week if you wanted."

I opened my eyes to find him watching me closely. My heart thumped happily. "Well…this is my home now, isn't it?"

His grin was immediate and gorgeous. "Right here." He leaned the inch between us and kissed me hard. "This is your home, Em," he growled happily and kissed me harder.

His palm skated down to my leg and he pulled, tugged, and gripped my thigh through my jeans. I had a feeling that Mason had a thing for legs because he paid an awful lot of attention to mine. He made me feel so loved, so welcome, so needed in that moment.

And he was completely right.

I trusted him, closed my eyes, and hung on for the ride.

Useless Fact Number Three

Only 24% of Americans do not have a tattoo.

Mason

I woke with my arms around her. I groaned at the feel of it and couldn't wait until this was a daily occurrence. I glided my hand down her side, past her hip to her leg, and back up again. She was so real in my bed— not a dream, not a cruel hoax my mind played on itself.

She was real.

She was here.

She was mine.

She trusted me.

She *wanted* me.

I closed my eyes and leaned over her, smelling her hair, knowing my pillow would smell that way after she was gone. That smell was imprinted in my senses. I'd know it anywhere.

I leaned back a little to see her face, brushing her blonde hair back, unable to stop the smile at the way she breathed and slept so soundly in my bed next to me. Even though my comforter was from Target and not Macy's, she still slept so soundly.

Christmas was tomorrow. I looked around my room. We had plans to go and bring a load of her stuff here. My room wasn't too bad. It had a bathroom attached and two big windows. I'm sure she was going to make it a lot cozier than I ever had. And we had decided that Milo's room wasn't needed anymore, so that was going to be cleaned out after the new year to make room for…whatever. I grinned at the thought that there might be another little boy in that room in a few years. This house that was always my home…

It was a shame we couldn't decorate for Emma's first Christmas here, but we kept everything the same for Mom so she wouldn't freak every time she couldn't remember.

But Emma's parents' house had enough decorations for an entire village, so that didn't really matter. Her brother and sister were coming the day after tomorrow, and we were all going to spend Christmas dinner together. And exchange gifts. It made me shiver with unease just thinking about that. I had no idea what to get people who already had everything, so that should be an interesting night.

I ran my knuckles across Emma's cheekbone. The softness didn't surprise me. She lay on her side facing me, one of her legs tucked snuggly between mine. I had been with only a couple women. Girls, I should say. In my teen party-football-crazy-fun days. I chuckled to myself at how stupid we were back then. Thought we were kings of our own little worlds. I didn't really date a whole lot. I had one steady girlfriend my junior year for a few months, but it wasn't the serious kind. It was just the fun kind, the kind where you went out on the weekends to movies and parties and then made out in the car afterward. We never exchanged 'I love you's; it was just fun. Insignificant. Inconsequential. When it wasn't fun anymore, we both moved on. And the couple of girls I'd *been with* were either stupid party hookups or crushes who saw an opportunity. My teen self was just happy to have a normal life with normal friends. We got into normal trouble and acted like normal, hormonal teenage boys.

There has never been a girl who made me want to bring her into my entire world, to live and breathe my air every day.

And then my life shattered and I never thought I would ever, ever have or want that again. You're not even the same person after guilt has eaten away at you for so long. I was so consumed with my mom and all the things that needed to be done for her that when I found Emma at that party, I literally felt a crack in my armor. And then more salty guilt was poured into the wound when I found out that she'd been hurt...because of me. Because I should have helped her, stopped her. But Emma showed me how life can heal the cracks in our armor with people put in our path.

They say what doesn't kill you makes you stronger, and I think Emma and I both are testaments to that.

I leaned in and kissed her lips because I couldn't leave the bed without doing it. Once, twice, and again as her lips puckered and she sighed in response. I slipped my legs away and off the bed before pulling the blanket over her, tucking her in. Her blonde hair framed her face and the pillow like the angel she was.

Last night she had been no angel, however.

I couldn't stop my grin. Last night had been particularly amazing and hard to keep a rein on. She was a wildfire and I was apparently surrounded by tinder. It's kind of funny how as teenage boys we tried to see how far girls would let us get, and instead with Emma, I was constantly trying to make myself stop. The wedding was only a week away. That was nothing compared to the time she'd lost and the time I'd wasted.

Yes, technically, we hadn't had sex. But yes, technically, we were both pretty content by the time we closed our eyes for the night.

With all the things that have happened, all the *firsts* that Emma lost with her memory, I wanted this first to be so memorable she'd never be able to forget. I wanted that night so ingrained in her that it could never be removed. I had a cabin for us in the mountains with no one and nobody around to disturb us. I had the nurses coming to help Mom round the clock, and they all understood how to care for her special circumstances.

I was so ready to give Emma that memory.

I pulled some clean jeans on from the drawers, slipping them over my boxers. I threw on a plain white t-shirt and peeked back at her to make sure she was still asleep as I slipped out. We stayed up pretty late last night, so it was late in the morning. I needed to do some exercises with Mom before we left for Em's parents to start packing up some of her things.

I turned the corner from the hall to find Mom in her chair, finishing up some oatmeal the nurse had given her. She smiled when she saw me, but then did a double take. It's the same double take and same shocked look in her eyes that I've seen every single day. "Mason, what…"

"Mom," I knelt down and put my hands on the tops of her knees, "you were in an accident, remember?" I ask, though I know she doesn't. "You lost your memory."

"I did?" she says, her eyes turning a little glassy. I pulled a tissue from the box by her chair. She went through several a day. I checked it often to make sure it was stocked.

"Yeah, Mom." I continued to explain it until she understood, and then I told her I was going to work her legs, like I did with her every day. It takes me about ten minutes to answer all her questions and explain everything so it sinks in.

I pulled her leg out straight before her, pull and release, pull and release to stretch out the muscle.

She began her grilling, like she did every time. "So your brother doesn't live here anymore?"

"No, Mamma." I don't tell her all the gory details of Milo because in a little while, she won't remember anyway. It's not worth getting her worked up over. "I graduated and went to school to be a physical therapy assistant so I could take care of you. We have a nurse who comes while I'm at work."

"Where do you work?"

I chuckled. "Inside Out Tattoo." She looked confused. "I own the place. I don't work with other patients anymore, just you."

She smiled wryly. "So you finally did it. You finally opened your tattoo shop."

I smiled back, switching legs. "Yes, ma'am."

Her smile changed. "You went to school to become a PTA for me, didn't you?" I didn't need to answer. She knew. "My Mason," she mused, "always trying to take care of me."

"It was only fair. You always took care of me." We didn't go into the accident. I tried once before, but couldn't do it. The old me hadn't wanted to hear that I wasn't to blame, and the me now just wanted to spend as much time with her as possible before she started to forget again.

She reached out at one point and tussled my hair. "Your hair." She laughed. "You look so grown up."

"I am grown up." I looked up at her as I pressed the pressure points on her feet. "I'm getting married in a week."

Her face was getting comical. Every day for weeks when I said that, she made almost the exact same surprised face. And she clutched her chest like she could die right there of happiness. The exact same way, every time. "Oh, Mason."

"Her name's Emma. She was one of my patients before I opened the tattoo shop."

"And she's fine now? She's OK?"

I nodded. "She is. She lost her memory, like you. But where as you can remember your life and only forget past a certain point, she lost everything." Sympathy swept over her features. "She could remember the world we live in, but not anything from her own life."

"Oh, my…"

"Yeah," I agreed.

"And now you're getting married. What if she remembers everything one day?"

"I really doubt she will. Not that I wouldn't want her to," I rushed on. "It's just not a probability. But even if she did remember everything, she would still remember what's happened since she woke up from the coma. I would hope she would still want me if that were to happen," I joked. "I am awfully hard to forget."

Mamma smiled and shook her head. "That's truer than blue."

"That will never happen," I heard from behind me. I looked over my shoulder at a well-rested, but slightly tousled Emma. Her head was tilted, her smile genuine and adoring. She was tugging at the hem of her shirt, waiting for what I was about to say. Mamma beat me to it.

"Mariah," she said, but it was almost a question. Like she didn't quite know.

"This is Emma, Mamma." I stood and went to Emma's side, picking up her hand and kissing her palm. I looked at her as I explained to my mother. "This is the girl I told you I was going to marry."

Emma had heard this speech several times already, but every time I said that I was going to marry her, her eyes leapt with life. It made me a very smug man to know that she wanted it as much as I did.

When we looked back to Mom, she had a strange look on her face. I knew she was probably forgetting, her mind digressing back to the safe zone it kept. But then she never changed, her face turned sad, mournful. "Mom?"

She was looking at Emma. "I've met you before, haven't I?"

Emma looked at me and then back at Mom. "Yes, ma'am."

"Tons of times, I bet. And every time, y'all have to explain to me who you are and I realize then that it's you. You're the reason my Mason looks so happy."

Emma laughed a little. "I hope so. He's doing an awful good job at doing that for me."

"I bet he is. He was always so good at taking care of things around here when his father left."

"You did an amazing job. He's…amazing." Emma smiled at me before going to the kitchen and yelling over her shoulder, "I'll get you some hot tea, OK?"

Mom looked at me. "She knows that I like my tea hot?"

"You and Emma get along great. She reads to you and y'all watch TV and talk."

"That's right," she said in surprise. "I was reading *Mansfield Park*, wasn't I?" She looked up into my eyes. "She reads that to me?"

"Every day," I said proudly.

Emma came back in and put the cup on the coaster for Mom. "There you go." Then she took the blanket from the chair and placed it across Mom's lap gently. "Are you both done with therapy? We can watch something for a little while before we go to my house. Ooh!" She turned in excitement and pointed the remote at the TV. "*It's a Wonderful Life* is on all day."

"Thank you, Mariah…Emma. Sorry."

Emma giggled. "Don't worry about it. I kind of like it now."

She was so good with my mom.

I stared at her and looked at the clock. Usually, Mom had digressed by now. And she never went too far into the things that have happened since. It was as if her brain knew that she would be forgetting it soon and kept a barrier there to keep her safe. But her barrier was down today and I didn't understand why or what that meant.

When Momma didn't say anything, we both looked at her. She looked up at Emma and then at me, her eyes no longer just glassy, they were full of tears that spilled over as soon as I recognized them.

"Mamma, what—"

"Come here, honey." She beckoned Emma to her. "Come here and hug me while I can still remember who you are."

Emma's face immediately crumpled into this strange combination of relief and sadness. She practically sprinted over to her, kneeling and falling into the cage my mother made with her arms. I watched as my mom let her hands travel the length of Emma's hair and then her cheek, memorizing her. Then she switched her gaze up at me. "I feel like I'm barely hanging on and could fall at any minute." A sob escaped. "I don't want to go."

I felt my heart slam inside my chest. She beckoned me to her. I couldn't move until she told me to. I caused this, and though I had let the guilt go, it still hurt when it came up like this and punched me right in the gut.

I knelt by Emma and Mom hooked her arm around my neck, almost to the point of pain, as she clung to us, clung to the present. She repeated, "I don't want to go. I want to stay here."

I barely held in my own sob and looked up at her, knowing she was going to be taken back into the past of her mind at any moment.

Emma leaned back and looked over at me, hopefulness climbing its way to the surface. I could see it in her eyes. I shook my head. It wasn't that I didn't want it. It wasn't that I didn't hope for it, but I had researched statistics and medical studies and miracle recoveries. She had been like this too long. I'd gotten my hopes up a couple times before with her, but I just knew…in my guts and heart and bones that whatever this was, it was a gift. Simply that. It wasn't here to stay.

I took Emma's fingers in mine as we sat at my mother's feet and rubbed my thumb over her knuckles. I looked up at Mamma and smiled in allowance as she rubbed my hair like she used to do when I was a boy.

"You call Emma 'Mariah' all the time," I started. "Do you know why you do that?"

She looked at Emma, but her eyes were far away. "I was in a sorority with a girl named Mariah. She looked an awful lot like you. But she's my age now, so she wouldn't look the same." She touched Emma's hair. "Her hair was the exact color of yours. Not quite wheat, not quite daffodil."Emma's smile showed she enjoyed that. "She was my roommate for two years, but a little bit too brazen for my taste."

Emma cracked up at that and resumed her rightful place—right up against me, her arm through mine.

We talked back and forth for a while and I made hot chocolate for everyone before ordering some delivery for lunch because Mamma was still with us and I was afraid to leave and lose it.

Then it happened. The thing Mamma and I had never talked about before. She asked me what happened with the accident. Emma gripped my hand tightly, silently telling me that it was OK and she wasn't going anywhere.

I didn't want to, but as I looked up at Mamma, I knew she deserved to know, even if she didn't remember it later. I told her what happened with the party and how Rick and I both were so drunk. I explained how he tried to leave in his car and I tried to stop him. When she got where the story was going and clutched her chest in an attempt to hold in the sob, I kept going. It all was spewing from the inside and once it started, there was no stopping it. It had to be said. It *had* to.

When I got to the part where I walked home and came upon the accident, how I grieved for my best friend for a full five minutes before I even recognized the mangled car as my mother's. How it hit me all at that moment that yes, I had let my friend die by not trying harder to stop him from leaving, and yes, I had pushed the domino over to cause the effect—the fact that she was also harmed by my actions. And then Milo left because of those same actions and it was all my fault. All of it.

Then I told her how that same domino effect had led me to Emma, and then I confessed something to them both that I'd never uttered out loud. That I felt even more guilty that my happiness in Emma had been found through all the actions before it. If I had not pushed that very first domino, Emma wouldn't be mine, would she? And then I went further and wondered what kind of life Emma would have had after she woke up and had to go back to living the life of the old her. She'd be with Andy and though she wasn't happy with him, he wouldn't have felt the need to kill himself. So, chalk that one up to me as well. The list of transgressions was a mile long, and I felt every inch of that mile right then.

With my mother's eyes on me, I felt raw. With my love's eyes on me that I could feel on the side of my face, I felt the stitches of the wound that Emma had closed with her love and understanding and acceptance begin to tug and pull.

Would she keep coming to my rescue when the past kept coming to find me? Even when I thought that I was fine and the past had been laid to rest? How many times would Emma have to come fetch me from the depths before she no longer could? Or worse…no longer wanted to?

Useless Fact Number Four

Peanuts are one of the ingredients in dynamite.

Mason

My mother snapped to bring me into the present. Her face was fierce, reminding me of the motherly, protective woman who used to take care of me. "Oh, Mason," she said harshly. "Do you honestly think that I was coming to get you because I thought you would drive drunk?" She shook her head and looked so disappointed in me. I deserved it. "Of course I wasn't. I knew you wouldn't drive drunk." I looked at her face and knew that she was about to rip my whole theory wide open. I braced myself for impact. "I trusted you. I knew you were being stupid kids and getting into trouble, but you were still a good kid. I knew you would never do anything to make me worry."

I shook my head. "No, Mamma. You got in the car and were coming to get me, to stop me from driving—"

"No, I wasn't," she argued, her eyes hard and fierce. "I knew you wouldn't drive. I was coming to get you because I didn't want you to have to walk, because I *knew you wouldn't drive*. I knew you'd be walking home

57

because your idiot friends would all be drunk, too. You couldn't reach me on the phone to come get you and I knew *you wouldn't drive*, Mason. Do you hear me?"

The ache in my chest hurt like an open wound. It was like tunnel vision. All I could focus on and hear was the echo of my mother's words. *I wasn't coming to stop you from driving, I was coming so you didn't have to walk home. Mason…. Mason. Mason!*

I snapped out of it to find Emma sideways in my lap, her hands on both sides of my face. I blinked. She looked like she didn't know what to do with me. I just wanted to feel her. I just wanted her to hug me to her-

She wrapped her arms around my neck and pressed herself to me, her lips in my hair. Without even thinking, my arms wound themselves around her. She knew what this was doing to me. For my mother to tell me that everything—entire years of hatred—was for nothing?

I leaned back a little and spoke to Emma's chest because I didn't want to face my mother. "Still, Mom. You still got in the car and were coming for me because you were worried about me. You—"

"I'm your mother, of course I was worried about you. That is my job." I finally peeked at her over Emma's shoulder. She looked like she wanted to take a switch to my behind. I gulped, not from fright from the woman who chased me with a switch on more than one occasion, but because even though I hated my guilt, it was almost like I was clinging to it. "For you to take the blame and say it was your fault because I was doing my God given duty and right?" She shook her head angrily. "You don't get to take that away from me, Mason."

"I'm sorry, Mamma." Emma moved from my lap and went around to my back. Her hands on my back urged me forward with light pressure. I followed her lead and let my mother wrap her arms around me the way she hadn't in years. She smoothed my hair like I was a little boy and I told her again that I was sorry. For now, I was sorry I hurt her. Soon, I hoped to be able to let it all go for good and be sorry that I had given her something for me to apologize for in the first place.

Emma took our mugs to the kitchen, I was sure, to give us a minute alone more than to keep things tidy. She stayed gone for longer than I liked, and I remembered what I'd said. About feeling guilty that the only way I had Emma was through all the things that had happened. That us finding each other was only a product of the crappy things I'd done.

I squeezed my eyes shut. Sometimes I was *such* an idiot. Emma and I weren't the product of guilt and transgressions. Emma and I were the light that peeks through all the blackness after the dust settles.

I knew she was feeling guilt over what I'd said. Another domino effect. I stood and said, "Need anything from the kitchen? Juice?"

"Juice," Mamma agreed and asked for a pen and a sheet of paper. She wrote a couple words down, folded the paper, and stuck it in an envelope. She asked me to stick it in the basket for mail to go out, so I did. She watched me go to the kitchen with a wistful smile.

I found Emma at the sink. She was rinsing the cups, looking out at the snow-covered picnic table in the backyard.

I put my arms around her stomach. She didn't jump, so I knew she heard me. I pulled her hair to the side and pressed my lips to the skin under her ear. She sighed and leaned back into me a little bit, even if she was upset with me.

"I'm sorry, baby." I kissed her skin again. "I didn't mean that I regret finding you or that everything we are was built on bad things."

"I know," she lied and turned with a teary smile that she tried to play off. "I know. And I know it was good for you to talk it all out with your mom. I hope you feel better about things."

"Emma," I steered us back on track. "I mean it."

"Mason, she's your mom," she reasoned and shrugged. "Of course if you have to pick meeting me or your mom never having the accident, you'd pick that. Of course you would."

"That's not what this is. It's not me picking that over you. I just felt…so guilty that…" She shuddered a little with the strain of holding in the sob. I felt like such a bastard. "It was all just spewing out. I'm sorry. I would never have said that to you. I just feel guilty sometimes that I can be so…happy with you, that I can't imagine ever having been this happy with someone else had the accident not happened that led me to you. It's like I'm…grateful."

She pressed her lips together. "I'm sorry. The way we met before my accident…it just all felt like destiny or something to me. It was more than just me loving you, it was like we…belonged. I thought what we have was good for you, to help push your past away."

"It is," I urged and took her face in my hands. "Please don't think for a second that it's not. I love you, Em. I love you so much and I wouldn't want this to go away for anything in the world. We're not made of bad memories, we're made of salvation. You saved me the day you woke up and I'll always be grateful to you for that."

She looked at my chest, not believing me. I sighed again at my stupidity. I hated that she felt like she was the cause of guilt for me. I lifted her chin and gazed into her gorgeous eyes for a few needed seconds before latching onto her mouth with nothing but love. And I'm sure a whole lot of reverence and adoration because I couldn't hide that. She kissed me back, but it was the first time that her heart and soul weren't in it. She didn't kiss me with abandon like she usually did. She kissed me back with doubt clinging to the edges.

I hated that I was the one to put it there.

My tongue licked at the seam of her lips, waiting for her to open for me. When she did, I felt some of that crumble away and succumb. The noise that escaped her was a sigh as much as it was a moan. I pulled back, kissing her slower and slower. Her cheeks were flushed and she looked so kissable that it was hard to pull away. I gave her a look to tell her we'd finish this later—the conversation and the kiss. With one final kiss to her forehead, I grabbed a bottle of juice out of the fridge and took Emma's hand, towing her with me so she couldn't stew in the kitchen.

When we entered, Mom's gaze swung to mine and her lips parted in surprise. "Mason? What happened to…"

I knew I'd lost her again. Though I would keep her with me always, this one long day to spend with her when it wasn't supposed to be medically possible, this one day to close the door on the regret and guilt, was worth it. The nurse had come in at some point and patted Mom's shoulder.

I sighed and felt a hundred pounds lift from my shoulders. My mother, the only person who could ever have given me the peace and forgiveness I thought I needed, but wasn't able to with her new mind, finally gave me that last little puzzle piece. I felt whole and light and though I missed my mom with a clear head, she would always be my mom. I needed to remember that though I took care of her, it was her job first, and she always did take care of us.

I turned to Emma with a smile to tell her I was sorry once again and that I felt really, truly free, but she was staring at Mom with teary eyes. My smile slipped away before she could even see it. "What's the matter, Em?"

"First, I make you feel guilty for loving me with all the steps it took to get to me…and now I've taken your mom's last minutes of clarity because you thought you had to come make me feel better."

"No, Em. We knew it wasn't going to last."

"But you could've spent it with her 'til the last second that she was here with you." She closed her eyes. One lone tear broke my heart.

"Em, don't. I'm OK. I got to spend all day with her-"

"Maybe I should have left and let you have it with her by yourself. Then you wouldn't have felt like you had to hold back."

I let a slow breath go. "I wanted you here with me. I wanted her to meet you and know exactly who you were and that I was going to be OK. That I found someone that made me happy."

"Yeah," she whispered. "Happy and guilty."

I didn't know what to say to her to get her to understand. She was so good at saving me from myself, and I apparently wasn't good at doing the same for her.

"Emma, it's been four years. Four years of self loathing." I cupped her cheek. "That takes a long time to undo. When you helped me see that my mom's accident was just that, an accident, that I couldn't take the blame for other people's actions? I understood and accepted it. But for some reason, it's hard to let go of it all. It still sticks and clings to things. I haven't been able to have a real conversation with my mom in four years, and not being able to talk to her about the accident, about everything, it all just came flooding back. It was like this was the final piece, the final straw, and now I can finally, finally be free of it. I guess I held on to a little bit of that self-hate and blame because only the person who I had hurt could set me free."

She nodded slowly. "OK."

"Em…" I heard myself growl low, "baby, you're everything to me. You're my saving grace, the very heart in my chest. I'm nothing but a hollow man with not a thing to look forward to without you. I thought that's what my life was going to be, and then you came bursting into my world and made all the color come back. You don't ever have to worry about where you belong, because you belong right here." I kissed her palm and then put her hand over my heart. "I'm so sorry that I made you doubt that."

She sniffed and I wiped the wetness away with my thumb. I had to fix this. I leaned forward, pressing my lips to her hair and whispered how sorry I was, over and over. "I'm sorry, I'm sorry, I'm sorry. Please forgive me, baby."

"Mason," she sighed and pulled back a little. "I believe that you're sorry." She licked her lips. "I'm going to go home and pack up some of my things, OK? You can come by later and help me, if you want."

My phone dinged with a text message. I didn't dare open it right then. "I can go now."

"Just stay here with your mom for a little bit."

My phone dinged again and she sighed, giving me an irritated look that I couldn't blame her for. I opened it up quickly. It was one of those stupid texts I'd been getting for months now that were to the wrong number.

You never gave me a chance.

Perfect timing, I growled to myself. Way to piss off Emma even more. I showed her so she'd know it was something inconsequential and didn't matter. I stuck it in my pocket and was about to tell her I'd get my coat when she beat me to it.

She looked over at Mom as the nurse took her blood pressure. "Just…be with her for a while."

I knew she just wanted to be alone. I was fine with that. As long as giving her space didn't mean that she was over-thinking. I kissed her lips once before she grabbed her coat and keys and headed to her car. She left her gloves, scarf, and hat, but I didn't say anything.

I stood in the frame of the door and watched her get in her car and back out. When she reversed out into the street and put it in drive, she paused and looked out her window at me.

I didn't like that pause.

I raised my hand to stop her, but she was already going. I sighed and rubbed my forehead. God, help me, I was stupid sometimes. I'd give her a little bit and then I was going after her. And she better be ready to swoon, because I wasn't letting her out of my arms until she understood that she was home in them.

Useless Fact Number Five

In the course of an average lifetime you will, while sleeping, eat 70 assorted insects and 10 spiders.

Emma

As soon as I pulled into the driveway, I got a call. I thought it was Mason and I wasn't really ready to talk about it again, but I looked anyway. It wasn't him.

"Hey, Mrs. Betty."

"Hey there." She sounded tired.

"You OK?"

"Oh, I'm fine. I've been working all day. I'm just getting off, but I thought there was something you should know."

"OK…"

"Adeline got fired. Remember your therapist?"

"How could I forget? What happened?" And why does it involve me?

"It's all very hush, hush," she said in a loud whisper. "But it turns out that she's been making all these weird phone calls from the office phone. Then the janitor found a huge stack of pictures and papers, letters, and…stuff in her office. They confronted her about it, and the next thing I know, *bam*. She packed up her office and left."

"OK. Well…that sucks, but what does that have to do with me?"

"Emma, the pictures…were of Mason. And her. And you. The letters were notes she wrote, letters to him that she never gave him, a journal type thing, things he said to her while they worked here, things he did to her-"

"What?" I breathed in agony. He told me there wasn't anything going on with—

"No, not like that. It said things like *Mason brushed me off today again. One day he'll go out with me.* Or *Mason is so naïve for falling for that little cheerleader.* Or…*Mason and Emma should run their car off Bigg's Cliff.*"

I scoffed. "OK," I said. I still wasn't sure what to make of it. "She's jealous. I'll keep an eye open."

"Good. I'm not saying you should get a restraining order or anything. I mean, she never did anything or contacted you, right?"

"No, never."

"OK. Well, be careful. I'm sure there's a good reason. With Mason, there always is. See you in a week." I could hear her grin as she hummed, "Dun, dun, duh, dunnnn."

I laughed sadly. "Thanks, Mrs. B."

We hung up and I started to get out, glancing in my rearview mirror on the way, but stopped. At the end of my driveway sat a red car. I got out and turned to look at it. Mrs. Betty had me paranoid now, of course, but I realized I wasn't paranoid at all when Adeline pressed the gas and drove by. She stared me down the entire time until she was out of view.

My heart beat faster. Oh, no. Was she about to be trouble for us? And how did she have pictures of her and Mason? Had Mason not told me something?

I reached inside the car to call Mason and tell him, but stopped. My calendar reminded me of my appointment in the next town over. I had completely forgotten with all the excitement of Mason's mom that I had to pick up his gift today.

My parents had set up college funds for me forever ago, so school was taken care of. However, they must have expected me to go to like Yale or something, because the community college's tuition for the year barely put a dent in that account. I told them I wanted them to take back the money I wasn't using, but they refused. They said working while going to school was stressful and they set the money aside for me for college. That included living money. When Mason proposed, I thought they might change their minds and take the money back, but no. Dad had written the check out to the college and given me bank cards for it before I could even ask.

And the first time I tried to pay them a payment for the Mini Cooper, they said it was paid off already. So, I had money for Christmas and they swore a million times it was perfectly fine. They were my parents after all. I was their daughter.

I stuck the phone back in my pocket and climbed back in the car. My phone dinged with a text just as I was pulling out.

I love you. So much. You know that right?

What timing. I smiled in spite of the situation. I looked both ways before backing out. I tried to tell myself I wasn't looking for Adeline's car, but I kind of was. I pulled up the text on my phone and spoke into the speaker for the talk-to-text, "I know. Why don't you come over in two hours. I'll be ready to go. We can talk. Love you."

I could get his gift real quick and then get back to the house, throw some things in a box, and he'd never be the wiser. I sighed and drove the distance to the shop in the next town.

As far as Mason's guilt…I honestly understood what Mason was saying, and I understood how he felt. But actually hearing with my own ears that loving me made him feel guilty? That didn't feel good. But I just had to make him see that he didn't need to feel that way about it. About *us*. And his mom today—what was that miracle about?

I skipped through town, my mind running a mile a minute. It took only about fifteen minutes to get to the next little town. I pulled into the shop I called weeks ago and really wanted to just sit and think, watch the snow for a minute while I thought of what to say to Mason later. I knew he was going to go overboard in trying to make me see that we were OK, everything was *OK*. He just still had a few things to work out in that amazing head of his.

And you know what? That *was* OK.

I remembered what it felt like to find out all the things that I'd done. I had felt like the guilt and blame was burying me. That doesn't change overnight. That doesn't just flit away to nothing just because you make the decision to forgive yourself and move on.

I took a deep breath and opened the door to the freezing Colorado air. I practically sprinted across the salt covered parking lot and into the store, cursing myself for forgetting my scarf and hat. I told the guy my name and he went and got a box from the back. He opened it and showed me with a little smile that said he knew I was going to be impressed. I smiled back.

I wasn't a tattoo artist, but even I could tell this thing was awesome. It was a custom Danny Fowler machine, and the man told me all about it, how he had one and it was his absolute favorite machine. I paid him and took the box with me, setting it in the passenger's seat like it was precious.

When I checked my phone, I had no texts or missed calls, so I hurried from the lot to get back to my parent's to pack. The snow was falling hard. The salt and snow trucks were running nonstop. I passed one at the last red light out of town before the stretch of long highway. Snow flew up on the side of his tractor into the ditches in waves. That much snow had fallen since I'd come through. I focused on the road and couldn't see any cars in front of me. I trekked on slowly and it hit me that sneaking off probably wasn't a good idea. I should have at least let someone know where I was going.

As if my phone had ears to hear me groaning about it, it rang. I opened it without looking to keep my eyes on the road, knowing it was Mason anyway.

"Hey."

"Emma."

I froze. It wasn't Mason. It was Adeline. I just knew it. "Adeline?"

74

"Now I have nothing," she whispered.

In my mind, I imagined her looming somewhere like she had at my house earlier. I swung my gaze all around in search of her and then, it happened.

You know when you get this gut feeling. When you just know that it's too late, and by the time you look, it's all happening in front of you in slow motion? You're amazed at how many things you can think of in just a few seconds. I was thinking that Mason would never know that I wasn't angry with him for what he said, but for the fact that there had apparently been something between Adeline and him and he didn't tell me. He was going to be eaten alive with guilt because we had a fight and he never got to make it all OK in his Mason way.

I watched the truck barely miss the snowplow, which was throwing huge waves of snow into the air, and swerve into my lane. I had nowhere to go but the trees. It was either plow into him and take him out with me, or let him go and take the trees alone instead, even though he hadn't given me the same courtesy. I held the wheel tight; my body knowing what my decision would be before I even gave it the command.

Mason.

That was all I could think. Please, God, don't let Mason's guilt be the end of him. Mason, I love you…

I didn't feel the trees as the car blew snow into the air in a big wave from the ditch before the trees sped toward me. I didn't feel a thing and I was grateful.

I closed my eyes and let the dark take me. I had spent six months of my life in the dark. I wasn't afraid of it.

And I wasn't afraid to die, I was just angry that I never got to *live*.

Useless Fact Number Six

Cherries will cause cancer cells to kill themselves.

Mason

When I pulled into her house a couple hours after she left mine, I was curious why her car wasn't in the driveway. The pavement was completely covered in snow, and the short drive over had been challenging, even for someone who had lived in Colorado all his life. My cell phone went off again with a text. I pulled it out quickly, but it wasn't Emma. I sighed as I read the message. I'd been getting messages all day that made no sense.

bastard.

That was it. *Bastard.* I even tried to call the number, but they didn't pick up. If it wasn't *bastard* it was *prick* or *jackass*. I'd been getting random texts for weeks now. No cause, no rhythm, only about once every couple of weeks, but they weren't violent until today. I showed Emma sometimes and we kind of laughed at some poor sap's misery. The ones before made me think that the person had the wrong number and was trying to text an old boyfriend or something.

I still think about you. Or *You didn't give us a chance.* Or *We could have been something.*

I shoved the phone into my pocket, giving the text no more of my thought or attention, and sprinted to the door, ringing the bell.

The butler answered as always, and when I asked him if Emma was there, he said no. She hadn't come home all day.

That sentence made my heart constrict. Normally, I would chalk it up to her out shopping or something, but now I was worried. She told me she'd be ready in two hours. What if she was just pretending she was all right and what I had said hurt her more than she let me know? She knew I was coming over…What if she was trying to avoid me?

I took out my phone and dialed her number. She texted me back just a couple hours ago saying she'd be here. The phone rang and rang with no answer. I texted her instead.

Baby, where are you?

When I got no answer, I texted again.

I'm so sorry for what I said. Please Em.

I stood in the doorway with Hanson for ten minutes waiting for Emma to answer me. I decided I'd wait for her in her room. Maybe I could help pack some things up while she was gone. Maybe my packing up would be a nudge for her to know that I wanted nothing more than for her to be with me, in my home, with all the family I had left. Though the storm had taken the idea to move right out of our hands. There would be no moving anything until this storm was over.

I told Hanson so and he nodded his approval, though I didn't need it. Isabella saw me heading for the stairs and cocked her head a little. "Mason. Is Emma back?"

"No…she said she was coming here to get a head start on packing some of her things, but that was a couple of hours ago and she's still not here."

"Why do you look so uneasy?" Her manicured hands went to her hips.

"We had a little…fight. But I thought things were OK."

She waved me off. "She'll be fine. Emma…the way she is, she doesn't hold on to grudges. I'm sure there's a explanation for why she's not here yet." She nodded up the stairs. "You can wait in her room if you like."

"If that's OK," I said, though I had been planning to do that anyway. Always the gentleman.

"Of course." She smiled and it was more genuine, the façade fading just enough to see it. "You'll be married in a week anyway."

I nodded and hoped that was still the case. I gritted my teeth at myself, wishing I hadn't said what I'd said. She squinted at me. "What happened with the fight? If I may ask."

"Just me saying something stupid." She continued to look at me, expecting me to go on. "I was telling my mom that I felt...guilty because Emma made me so happy. That I shouldn't be so happy about something that only came to be because of what happened with my mom's accident."

She raised her brow, not understanding why my mom had anything to do with it. I sat down on the bottom stair. She sat beside me. I looked at her face, to make sure the woman that I came to know when Emma was asleep was with me, not the one who showed up afterwards and caused Emma so much heartache fighting her own grief. When I saw it was indeed the woman I'd brought coffee to almost every day for six months, my guts spilled wide open.

I told her everything. She listened and put her hand on my knee in sympathy. I explained to her that I was over it, for the most part. I mean, you're never *really* over something like that, but when my mom asked me about the accident, my guts spilled to her, too.

She didn't seem surprised by what I'd said except that Emma would have gotten so angry that she wouldn't come home because of it. The clock said it was almost seven. It had gotten dark an hour ago.

And then the lights went out.

Her breath caught as I heard the fans of the appliances whir to a stop, the house quieter than I'd ever heard it. "Oh, my. The snowstorm must have knocked the power out."

I pulled my phone from my pocket and pointed it around. Hanson came through with a flashlight, asking if we were OK. I rolled my eyes in the dark where no one could see me, as if the power going out could hurt us somehow. He gave a flashlight to Isabella and she went, spouting something about getting candles out. I looked at my phone with very little battery left and dialed Emma's number slowly to calm myself. I was trying not to freak about it. I normally wouldn't, Emma could do anything she wanted, but if the storm had gotten so bad the power went out, then I was now worried about her safety.

Mad at me or not, she needed to come home.

The call wouldn't send. The line told me that my call couldn't be completed and my heart sank into my stomach with dread. I went to the window and watched the wind whip the white flakes by in the minimal light the moon provided. I took my phone out once more and tried her number. Still no cell service or busy circuits or whatever was going on. I gripped the keys in my pocket and started to move toward the door when Rhett called my name from the den.

"Mason." His voice seemed surprised that I was there. "Oh, good. I was hoping you and Emma hadn't gotten caught in the storm somewhere."

"It's just me." I gulped and moved to the door once more. "Emma never came home after she left my place. I can't reach her by phone, and she should be here. I'm going after her." I opened the door. The wind and snow pulled the door from my grasp and slammed it against the foyer wall.

He called my name louder and ran to the door, just as I stepped onto the porch. "Mason, no. You can't go out in this."

"If Emma is out there, I need to find her. What if she's stuck somewhere?"

He looked at the snow with wide eyes. It wasn't the quiet kind that fell and seemed to bring a peaceful silence with it, it wasn't the kind that fell fast like rain and whipped in the wind. No, this was a storm in the truest sense. And with the look of horror on Rhett's face…*Emma's father's face*…I knew he realized I was right. "I'll come with you."

"I think you should stay. I'm going to check on Mom and the nurse, and then drive around and see if Emma broke down somewhere or got stuck. If she comes home and the phones still don't work, put a flare out or something so I know when I drive by that I don't need to keep looking."

He nodded slowly. "I have some flares in my tackle box in the garage."

I nodded and left without another word. I didn't want to sit there all day and debate about it. I climbed into the truck and backed out into the dark road. The headlights seemed to come out of nowhere. I slammed on the brake, sliding a little in the salted, snowed driveway. The driver went by at a snail's speed, so I decided to go the other way around the neighborhood, hoping to beat them to the main road. I understood the cautiousness. It was pitch black, the headlights just illuminated the snowfall piling on my windshield making it glow and blind me, the worst thing I'd ever driven in.

But I wasn't stopping.

I knew right then where I was going first after I checked on Mom. To pull into the police station after only a few hours of her being "missing" may be going overboard in normal circumstances, but not today. Not right now.

All I could think, breathe, and feel was protectiveness for my Emma. Something inside me was pushing me to her.

It was dark and I could barely see in front of me as it was, let alone look for a car on the side of the road, or parked somewhere. She didn't really have any girlfriends in this town. She was still working on things, friends being one of them. She had cut the cord with the school friends she had because they would not get past her past, which she had to do, so she didn't need them around her. Still, I hadn't heard her say much about any one person, so I couldn't imagine she'd be at someone's house. Unless she hadn't told me about them.

My brow lowered. Surely she would tell me if she had a friend that she hung out with sometimes, right? She would at least talk about them.

I searched out the window on the shoulder of the road and the ditches, and then sidewalks and parking lots as I got into town. I did drive by the shop first, just to make sure she hadn't gone there either.

No cars were parked out front. My heart sank and I hadn't realized how much hope I had put into that thought. So, I started to pull out toward the police station. I didn't see anything, and then all of a sudden, a car was right there. They honked and crawled by slowly. It was dangerous to be driving right now and I gripped the steering wheel tighter at the thought of Emma getting hurt somewhere and having no one to help her.

The short ride to the police station took longer than I wanted. It was dark, but I hoped someone was still there.

A couple of emergency lights were on in the back of the outdated and musky building, and I told the only man there behind the desk what was going on. What he had to say didn't make me a happy man. He said he was sorry, but he was sure lots of folks hadn't made it home in the storm and had family worried about them.

"Sir, I understand that, but I'm telling you that it's not like her. She said she was going straight home. It's only a few minutes from my house and she wasn't there. Never made it home."

"It's dark now. There's nothing we can do. Plus, it hasn't been twenty-four hours. We don't consider them missing until—"

My blood boiled. "She's not missing, she's in trouble!" I bellowed. We were wasting precious time.

I leveled him with a look and let it all hang out. I wanted him to see my anguish, my fear, my tortured guts. "Please, sir."

He sighed. "It's Christmas Eve. There's not anybody else even working tonight and they definitely won't be working tomorrow."

"You can go home to your wife tonight, knowing that you did nothing to help a girl that was in trouble, no matter what day of the year it was?"

He sighed again, in resignation this time. "Look, I'll take a Jeep with the spotlight out and look for her."

"Thank you," I said, not hiding my gratitude.

"Go on home and I'll stop by—"

"No," I said hard. "I'll look, too. I'm not going home just to let you look by yourself. I think that would be pointless."

"It's not safe out there," he told me, slipping on his coat and hat. "You'll be safer at home—"

"No. I know it's not safe. It's not safe for Emma if she's caught out there somewhere in the storm." He gave me a look. "I'm not going home."

He sighed as he opened the door. "My cell's not working. I'm sure yours isn't either. Meet me back here in two hours, whether you've found the girl or not. That's the only way I'll do it. If you don't find her, you're going home to start again in the morning with some light. I mean it."

I nodded, though I wasn't sure I could do that.

The first place I went was the hospital. I…hated to do it. I didn't even want to think about it, let alone actually go there and see if she'd shown up, but I asked the nurse at the desk. They were writing down names of people who had come in since the computers weren't on the emergency power system. She assured me no one by that name had been brought in. So I started searching again. After an hour of circling highways in the heavy snow, I started to let my mind wander to other possibilities. Maybe she had gone out of town. I had no idea why she would, but what if she had? There were several ways out of town and it would take hours to search the roads if that was the new plan.

I beat my fist on the steering wheel and cursed loudly. I yelled some more because I just needed to. I pulled over into an abandoned lot and laid my head on the steering wheel.

I had an awful feeling that I was right and she wasn't on the main roads.

And then my cell phone rang. I gasped and picked it up. "Emma!"

"Mason," a familiar voice crawled through the line, sounding upset.

"What do you want, Adeline?"

"I called Emma." I could hear her fast breaths. "Something happened."

"Why the hell did you call Emma?"

"To…mess with her. Piss her off. Tell her about us."

Ice raced through my veins. "You what?" I said, dangerously low. "Us? There is no us!"

"I got fired today."

"I don't care."

"I got fired because they found pictures of us in my office."

"Pictures…of us?"

Adeline and I had one date. One. It was before Mom's accident, back when I was that stupid teenager who haunted me in more ways than one. We had gone to one of my friend's parties. Adeline went to school in the town over. I couldn't remember any pictures taken of us there, but who knew. That was the only way she could have pictures of "us". I was drunk that night and all I really remembered was that Adeline kept trying to drag me up to the rooms and I kept refusing. I told her that I wasn't looking for a girlfriend and she said she didn't care; she just wanted to have a good time that night. A *really* good time. And then my stupid teenage hormones caved, like an idiot. We had sex in the laundry room of my friend's house, of all places, and I regretted it about as quickly as it had begun.

She acted like it was no big deal. I never called her again because in my mind, we didn't have a great time and we barely said two words to each other the whole night. All she wanted to do was grind against me and beg me to dance with her. When I tried to ask her about what she was going to do that summer, she said she didn't want to ruin the moment with talking, just dance. I knew then my mistake had been grave and figured she wasn't that interested in me either. I thought would never hear from her again.

But I did.

When the texts came too frequently for me to ignore anymore, I told her as nicely as I could that I wasn't interested and for her to move on to someone else. That we just hadn't meshed.

She tried calling a few times a day after that, so I started leaving my phone at home… I sucked in a quick breath as I remembered. I had completely forgotten about that. I left my phone at home the night of Mom's accident because of Adeline…

"Mason? Can you hear me?"

"I hear you," I growled. "And I still haven't heard a good reason for why you called Emma." I closed my eyes tightly, my guts twisting. "If she got angry because of what you said, didn't come home because of it and got hurt in the storm, I'll—"

"That's what I'm trying to tell you." Her voice was small. "I didn't say anything to her about us. I just called and as soon as she picked up and said hello, there was a lot of screeching and noise. I think she may have wrecked her car or something."

My breath caught painfully. "Where was she?"

"I don't know."

"Why are you calling me?"

"I wanted to tell you. I just wanted you, Mason. I wasn't trying to hurt her and wasn't going to. I didn't mean to hurt anyone. I just wanted to make your life hell."

I hung up. I was not going to argue about what happened back then. If Adeline could call me, then I could call Emma.

I dialed, but she didn't pick up. I jerked the truck into drive and barely looked before jamming the gas and heading back down the road. I had no idea where Emma would have gone if she was angry with me about Adeline, but Adeline told me Emma had gotten in an accident. I couldn't think of anything Adeline would have gained from confessing that.

I *had* to find Emma now.

I shook my head violently. Could I realistically blame Adeline for Mom's accident and now Emma's, if that was the case? No, but she sure as hell had a hand in it.

I rounded the corner to Emma's neighborhood and passed her house. There were no flares lit and I felt my eyes sting. Oh, God, please. Don't let this happen…

All the breath left me at once when I looked at the clock and saw how late it was. It was almost time to meet the deputy, but there was no way I was going back there without finding Emma. I just…couldn't.

And then I remembered that he had a family waiting for him, too. They were probably worried about him. I'd make one more sweep and then meet him, but I wasn't going home. He could forget that.

I came to the end of the subdivision and started to turn right toward town, but stopped. I looked left, toward the road near the bridge. Emma had almost lost her life there once and Andy had taken his own life there. I didn't think Emma would go there, even if she was angry with me, but I felt my hands turning the wheel left and my foot pressing the gas anyway.

When I came to it, it was as I expected. No cars were there, no tracks, but that didn't matter since the snow covered it right back up. I drove over it and started looking for a place to turn around. I stopped and backed into a driveway. As I looked to the right to check for someone coming, I saw headlights. I waited, rubbing my face in anguish. I pressed my forehead to the steering wheel and closed my eyes so tight they hurt.

I couldn't bear the thought of not finding her tonight. My guts twisted painfully. At first, I thought I'd throw up from it. My eyes stung behind my eyelids and I realized my body was preparing me for the worst. I ripped off my seatbelt and got out, almost slipping with my leap from the cab. I kicked at the back tire and beat my gloved fist on the side of the truck. It didn't matter, the fabric ripped and it stung, but I kept hitting it until it hurt so bad that I knew the skin was ripped to the bone.

I stood there in the snow that had seemed to die down a little and listened to the quiet. The eerie quiet that snow provides settled around me, pushed in me and through me. I knelt down and let my aching fist rest on the snow to ice it. The quiet was practically yelling it was so silent. I slowed my angry breathing and tried to think, tried to find the answer that I knew I would regret later for not getting right.

I looked around at the snow-covered trees and land. I had been wrong. My body hadn't been preparing me for letdown. It felt not like I should give up, but that I should listen. I should pay attention, let my fear ebb away, and focus. Just like I used to tell Emma.

Never give up. Never let your fear and frustration cloud your focus.

I sighed, pulling my now numb hand from the snow. I stood and looked out at the road. The headlights were still sitting there and hadn't come past me. I hadn't been paying attention. I watched carefully. They weren't moving, but were muted behind all the haze the snow created.

And the snow and wind was picking back up again. It was stupid, I knew, but I let the hope creep back in that this was a sign of some sort, that the calm that had taken me over was letting me find the girl I was in love with.

I squinted at it before climbing back into the truck and making my way to it a little faster than I should have. The hope glowed in my chest. The car was facing my way so whoever was in there was coming towards town. The front end was wrapped around a tree, but the lights still shown on both sides. The car was completely covered in snow.

I swung the truck around to park by the ditch and jumped out. I couldn't make out the car with the way it was, but I knew, I just knew it was Emma.

I slid when I ran down the ditch and felt the freezing snow seep into the back of my jeans, but I got up, ran up the slope, and around the car to the driver's side door. I could hear music faintly, but the car was off. I knocked, but heard nothing. I furiously wiped away the snow from the window and door, but it was iced over. I bit into my fist to stop from smashing it through the window.

I cursed and growled all the way down to my soul, hating that everything had to have an obstacle. I searched for something to smash the window with, kneeling in the snow and shoving my hands down through it trying to find the ground. When I literally reached pay dirt, I pushed around, looking for a limb or rock. The snow was up to my upper arms and they were already turning numb.

I couldn't find a single thing to grab, so I labored back through the snowy ditch and opened my toolbox in the back of my truck. My numb fingers poorly gripped a wrench and I made it back to the car on adrenaline alone because I was fading fast. My arms were numb and my legs were too, and wet. I knew it wouldn't be too long and I'd be useless and in trouble myself.

I went to the back window to keep the flying glass from Emma in the front, reared back with as much force as I could muster and rammed it straight through the ice and glass. I sliced my arm when my hands went through the window with the force, but didn't even have time to look at it. I kept hitting until the entire window was gone and then kept beating down the side of the car to shatter the ice around the door so I could open it and get her out.

It fell almost soundlessly to the snow. I used my shoe with numb toes inside to kick and shove the snow

96

aside enough to wedge the door open, which took some time. When I finally got the door open enough to get in, blasted with her music that was still playing, I crawled in and there she was. My heart was leaned over in that seat, pale as the snow that raged outside, and blood on the side of her head.

My heart was fearful, but my body knew what to do as it reached out to touch her. She was ice cold. "Emma?"

My fingers were too numb to feel her pulse. My breath made thick fog, so I knew hers should, too. I watched closely, holding my breath so as not to mistake it for hers as I palmed her cheek.

"God, please…" I groaned and closed my eyes, unable to look until I begged. I closed them tighter and then opened. I watched and waited. When the barely there puff of breath came from her parted lips, I'd never been so grateful of anything in my life.

I undid her seatbelt and pulled her through the middle console to me in the backseat. With her in my lap, I kissed her ice-cold face and neck over and over as Royal Teeth played in the background. But I didn't have time to catch my breath. I had to get her to the hospital and hope to hell they had enough power to do what needed to be done.

I pushed the door open as far as it would go and slipped out from under her to get out. She moaned and I stilled. "Emma?" I palmed her cheek once more. "Baby?"

She moaned again and whispered her words. "Mason…the heater's on." She tried to pull at her jacket.

I didn't laugh. I knew that hallucinating was a bad sign when it came to hypothermia. I leaned over and hoisted her up into my arms as gently as I could muster. I trekked through the snow as fast as my legs would go, which wasn't very fast at all in the thick snow. When I finally reached the passenger door, I leaned her against the side of the truck just enough for me to get the door open. I stepped up on the rung and hoisted with everything I had left. She barely cleared the edge of the seat and I thanked the big guy for me getting her in the first try. I pushed her butt with my hand until she was clear.

I was spent. The cold was too much. My legs were no longer just numb, they were painfully so. I pushed her legs into the floorboard and shut the door. Leaning on the truck side, I made my way to the driver's door and gingerly climbed in. I had left the truck running and moaned feeling the heat on my hands as I put them in front of the heater.

I pulled Emma to me, setting her head and shoulders in my lap to try to keep her warm as I drove. My cold feet didn't want to cooperate, but I forced them to press the pedals and go. I needed to get there fast, but couldn't chance us getting in an accident. We'd never make it if something happened now.

Cautiously, I crossed the bridge and turned back onto the main road. My hands shook the entire time and I clamped my mouth shut to stop my teeth from banging. Emma's teeth didn't chatter and that scared the hell out of me. She didn't shiver, which meant severe hypothermia had set in. I drove a little faster.

When we got closer to town, I noticed the snow had let up a bit. By the time we reached the hospital, we weren't the only ones in the ambulance bay looking for help. I got out and pulled Emma from my side of the truck into my arms. She fell limply, not once opening her eyes or making a sound. I ran, leaving my door open and the truck on.

I kissed her head as I made it past the door because I knew they were going to take her from me. And I wasn't her husband yet, if she even wanted me to be anymore, so they wouldn't tell me a thing about her progress.

"Hey! Help me. Please," I called and the same nurse who I'd seen earlier came around the counter.

"You found her. Where?"

"In her car. She had an accident." She looked at Emma's eyes, prying open the lids. She touched Emma's lips that I could see had a bluish tint now that we were in the light. "Out past the bridge."

"How long has she been unconscious?"

I sighed. "Lady, I don't know. Just help her, please."

She sighed, too. "Bring her back here. There's not that many staff on tonight and it's too dangerous to drive in that." She gave me a look. "So, we're short staffed. You OK to help me?" She squinted at me. "No, no, you're not OK." She looked at my arm where the blood was and then my face. "You've got mild hypothermia it looks like."

"She's full-blown," I argued and followed her back to a room. "I don't care about me. Help her."

"You need stitches," she argued back as I placed Emma gently on the bed. "And a warming blanket and to get out of these wet clothes." She turned and grabbed something from a drawer. "Here." She tossed me a sheet. "Wrap this around you and then come back. I'll stitch you up later, but you at least have to get out of those wet clothes."

The only reason I was able to go into the bathroom was because the robust woman had already begun taking Emma's clothes off with skillful hands that knew exactly what they were doing.

I labored through it as fast as I could, the pain from my frozen feet and legs overriding the pain from my wounds, and wrapped the flimsy sheet around myself. When I came out not two minutes later, she had a metallic blanket over Emma and was tossing other blankets on top of that.

She looked at me. "All right, get in here, sport."

"In here?" I asked, but couldn't take my eyes off my Emma.

"Yes, in here." She lifted the side of all the blankets. "I assume it's you who put that pretty little rock on her finger, so it's you who's getting naked to warm her up, not me. Skin to skin, so take the sheet off."

She didn't have to tell me again if it was what Emma needed. I'd never seen Emma naked before and climbed in without a view even if I did want one. She was an ice cube. "Ah, Em, baby. You're freezing."

I stuck one of her legs between mine and pulled her arm to lay over my side while I wrapped her as closely as we could get.

"A lot of the machines are down because the generator is having problems, and I don't have anything to warm her with." She let me get situated before going on so the rustling would stop. "I don't even know if she's passed out from the hypothermia or the concussion. So we're going to run some tests. On you, too," she said sternly. "And you just lay there and keep her warm for me."

No problem.

I nuzzled my nose into Emma's face and breathed her in. Even like this, she still smelled like her. I picked her freezing hand off my side and put it between my palms. I blew my hot breath on her fingers. The nurse saw me and smiled as she looked at Em's head wound. When she pulled out stuff for sutures, I scowled. "Aren't you going to get the doctor?"

"I am the doctor," she spouted wryly. "I always work on holidays because I'm not married. It doesn't seem fair to their kids that they have to work, so here I am."

She pulled one of Em's arms from the blankets and started the fastest IV I'd ever seen. She smiled at my awe and taped the sensors for the monitors to Emma's fingers. "I've had lots of practice. I was a nurse before I was a doctor."

"How many of you are working tonight?"

She grimaced a split second, but I caught it. "There's only two doctors here and six nurses. The rest, we can't reach and they don't know to come...or can't get here."

I sighed. "It's a mess out there."

"It's a mess in here. I'm sure they'll trickle in as they can be found." She locked eyes on me as she put Em's arm back under the blanket. "Good thing you got here when you did."

I nodded. "Yeah."

"You know you saved her life, right?" I looked away, but she continued. "Like, seriously saved her life. She wouldn't have lasted much longer out there."

"I hope she agrees with you when she wakes up," I muttered, sweeping Emma's hair off her cheek as she faced me.

"Lover's quarrel?"

I closed my eyes and pulled Em as close as I could get her. "We'll see." I focused on Em's face. "Why isn't she warming up?"

The monitor started to beep faster. The doctor stopped what she was doing and looked at it.

"It takes a while for the body temperature to go back up. Her organs were already shutting down."

It beeped faster and faster. I held my breath, hoping that damn beep slowed back down, but it didn't. And when the doctor yelled for me to get up and move, I knew it wasn't going to. I pulled away from Emma as easily as I could and wrapped the sheet around my bottom half as I got up, scooting around beside her head.

And then the line on the machine betrayed us both by flat-lining, screaming for all to hear that my baby was dying on that table.

Useless Fact Number Seven

A teaspoon of honey is the life's work of 12 bees.

Emma

Someone was begging for my life. "Please, please, please don't take her. Please don't punish her for my mistakes. If it's not one part of my past creeping up, it's another and Emma always suffers because of it. Please, please."

Mason. I could feel his lips at my ear, his warm breath that felt so inexplicably good on my skin. Then his voice faded and I couldn't hear him. I strained for him, not knowing anything in that moment other than I needed him. Then the worst pain I'd ever felt blasted through my chest, burning my skin and scalding my veins.

"Emma, come back, baby."

I gasped awake, becoming aware of how painfully hot I was. Or…cold. I couldn't tell anymore. And how hard my heart was beating, as if doing its own begging.

Mason came into my line of sight from behind my head. He smiled, yet I could tell it was anguished, and put his forehead to mine. "Thank you, thank you. I'm so sorry, Em."

I wanted to speak, but couldn't. I barely held on to the thin thread of lucidity. I heard them speaking around me, a woman yelled at Mason and then I was engulfed in warmth. I tried my hardest to snuggle into it. Mason's arm came around me, his legs pulling me toward him and crushing our bodies together. It was so warm I could do nothing but sigh against his neck.

He kissed my eyes, my forehead, my hair. When he started to whisper to me, I knew that he knew...that I knew about Adeline. "God, help me. I don't know if you can hear me right now, but I'm so sorry, Em. I wasn't trying to hide anything from you. In my mind, there just wasn't anything to tell. It was one date, and that was it. I didn't know that she was holding onto…whatever she thought was between us."

I managed a small moan. I didn't want to talk about Adeline right then. I wanted to drown in his warmth. I didn't care what he did or didn't tell me in that moment. I just knew that somehow, someway, I had thought I was going to die in those woods, yet here I lay with Mason in reach. Nothing else mattered in that second. He must have known what I wanted, because he shushed me and pulled me as close and tight as he dared. He leaned down and tenderly kissed my lips. I heard murmurs from people around us as my arm was moved. I felt a stick before my veins were flooded with warm liquid. It made me feel as if I were floating. The pain started to go away and the tired feeling wasn't just knocking at the door anymore, it was coming in.

"Sleep, baby," he whispered into my hair as I felt warm fingers on my temple before a stick there, too. "I'll be right here."

And then I was out.

When I woke next, I was no longer wrapped around Mason. And I was no longer naked and freezing under my blanket. I had on a hospital gown and socks on my feet. The pounding in my head hit me the first inch I moved. Good Lord, it hurt. When I went to move my hand up to investigate, it was occupied. I pried open my eyes and looked over at Mason. He was sitting in the chair, his head on the bed beside me with both of his hands gripping mine. I brought my free hand up, ignoring the pull of the IV, and rested it on his head.

I wondered how long I'd been asleep. And for a few panic-filled seconds, I wondered if I had been in another coma, but if that were the case, Mason wouldn't still be sleeping here every night…would he? I shook my head. I remembered everything from my accident. I was fine except for the drum in my temple.

Letting my fingers rake his hair, I wondered what I was going to say to him. Finding out about Adeline wasn't what I'd wanted, and yes, I had been angry with Mason when I first found out. But as Mason lifted his head, I knew then that I didn't need to say anything. The man was torturing himself enough for the both of us.

Oh, my… His eyes were red and rimmed with irritation, like he'd been crying. His lips parted in surprise at finding me awake. "Hey, you," he said gruffly.

"Hey, you," I whispered back.

"Em." He scooted forward a little in his chair, but kept my hand in his. "Gah, baby. I'm so sorry." His chest heaved, catching the sob right on the edge. "How do you feel? Other than the obvious hell."

I croaked, "I'm all right. Just so tired."

He saw the struggle I was having with trying to sit up. He pressed the button for me and stopped when I was almost upright. We stared at each other, a whole conversation of worry, guilt, hope, and concern between us.

I cleared my throat and went to speak, but he shook his head softly, rubbing his thumb over my knuckles. "Wait. Just let me get this all out. It's been eating me alive since we got here." I nodded and licked my dry lips. "I didn't mean anything I said. I may have thought I believed it," he shook his head, "but I didn't realize how much I still let my guilt take me over sometimes." He looked me straight in the eye and choked on his words, as his eyes turned glassy. "I love you, baby. Loving you doesn't make me feel guilty. It feels like a miracle, like something I've got to grab onto and tighten my grip to make sure it doesn't get away. I don't regret loving you, and I wouldn't change anything. If you've taught me something, it would be that things happen for a reason." He gulped. "As hard as that is to accept sometimes, like right now while I'm looking at you so tore up in this bed, I have to believe that there's a reason for it." His eyes wandered to our hands, his thumb still rubbing my knuckles so adoringly. "Otherwise, I'll just go crazy. I have to believe that it all means something, otherwise you wanting me could be just a fluke, too, and I couldn't handle that."

He finally let his eyes settle back to mine and I felt the impact of that gaze. I couldn't look away if my life depended on it. "I not only want you, baby, I need you. You make me capable of being the person I was always supposed to be. And not only do I want you and need you, I choose you, because there's no one else I want to wake up with. And the Adeline thing? It wasn't even a thing at all. We went on one date a few years ago. She got a little clingy afterwards, but eventually stopped all together. I worked at the hospice before she did. When she started working there, you were already there. I wasn't about to leave you there because of *her*. Besides, I thought it was all behind us. It wasn't until the petty crap she tried to pull on you that I knew she wasn't over it. But it didn't matter. She asked me out a few times, but I wasn't interested. I love you, Em." He leaned down and kissed my fingers. "Please, please forgive me. I'm not saying that I won't ever mess up again, I'm sure I will, but I promise you that I'll do everything I can to make up for it. For the rest of our lives."

Obviously, tears were on the loose after that. The look he was giving me looked like he wanted to wipe them away himself, but he stayed put, as if scared of what I might have to say to his speech. I used my free hand to wipe under my eyes and looked at my lap. "Can I just ask why you didn't tell me about Adeline?"

He sighed a little, but said quickly, "Because she wasn't who I was focused on. Like I said, it was just one night with her years ago and it wasn't something I thought about. I didn't even think it mattered. But when you asked me if there was anything going on with Adeline, I should have told you then, but I didn't want you to think it was more than it was and worry about that. There was never anything with her. She's just a pathetic girl who couldn't let it go and tried to cause trouble." He ground his jaw. "I can't believe she called you to make it seem like…"

I remembered. She had called me in the car. But how did he know that? "How did you know Adeline called me?"

"She called me when I was out looking for you." What? He came looking for me? "She was the one who had been texting me those times, I'm pretty positive. She told me she had called you to mess with you, but there had been a accident or something and she wanted to let me know in case you were in trouble."

"The police didn't bring me here?"

He shook his head. That bashfulness that kept him so grounded surfaced, making me melt with the warmth of it. "I did. I…drove around looking for you when you didn't make it to your parents'."

My heart slammed. "You came out in the storm-"

A woman wearing a Santa hat came through the door before I could finish. She smiled at me and then smiled at Mason. "How did you sleep, hero?"

Hero? He chuckled and shook his head. "I'm fine. I want you to tell me that *she's* fine," he said and looked at me.

"Well," she spouted and looked into my eyes with a light, "she's not freezing to death anymore, so that helps things, right?"

"What?" I heard myself say.

She turned her curious gaze to me. "What do you remember about the accident?"

"Just…that. The snowplow was coming and a truck came around him. I had nowhere to go but the trees."

"That's it? You don't remember Mason bringing you in?" I shook my head. She smiled and proceeded to tell me how Mason had been looking for me for hours out in the snowstorm. How he went to the police and the hospital refusing to quit until he finally found me. Then how he smashed the ice around the car with a wrench to get the door open to retrieve my freezing body, almost freezing to death himself in the process.

"When he carried you in, he had mild hypothermia himself, and you, my dear," she smiled again, "were knocking on death's door. Literally." She shot a look at Mason. "We had to bring you back once. And then Mason laid in the bed with you to warm you up until you were stable."

I swung my gaze over to Mason. He had been watching my face the entire time, and now, he gulped and didn't look away. He looked heartbroken and concerned. I didn't understand why he'd feel heartbroken. I was all

112

right, I was right here…unless he thought I wasn't going to forgive him.

I squinted at him. Yeah, it sucked that he didn't mention Adeline. And yeah, it hurt when he said that he felt guilty loving me. But those weren't deal-breakers. Didn't he know that? I tilted my head and watched his thumb as it caressed the backs of my fingers. He didn't, did he? He honestly thought I was going to leave him, to break off everything, because of this.

We were supposed to be getting married in less than a week. I couldn't let him think that for another second because he had saved my life, risked his own life for me, and then stayed here with me all night, keeping me safe and warm…and he sat there thinking I was going to leave him.

I leaned forward as much as I could, grabbing his arms and pulling him to sit on the bed beside me. His arms stayed loose and tentative at our sides, unsure of my motives, but I reached around his neck and held on for dear life as I burst wide open.

Everything that I wanted for myself was right here in this bed with me. I didn't care if the nurse was there. I needed Mason more than I needed my dignity right then. I loved and hated the fact that he had risked his life for me. It was such a strange contrast.

I whispered in his ear through my sobbing throat, "I love you."

It was then he let himself go. All his muscles released and his arms, though careful, engulfed me with his warmth. With me pressed into his chest, he lifted one of those big warm hands and cupped my cheek, his thumb running over my lips as he rested his head to mine. I could practically taste the gratefulness coming from him. He had bandages on his arm and his hands. I ran my fingers over them gently, telling myself I'd ask him later. They were new, so I knew it had been from his search of me.

He got hurt for me even while he thought I was so angry I was going to leave him forever.

I heard the door close somewhere behind him, but we stayed like that. When he felt my tears on his hand, his intake of breath was slow. "Baby," he soothed. "Shh."

He pressed and rubbed my entire body in intervals of warm pressure. He even rubbed down my legs and back up again. With my face buried in the crook of his neck, and my arms around him as much as I could get them with wires and tubes, I cried for the way he loved me and somehow always found blame within himself that he wasn't good enough. I knew right then he was blaming himself, thinking that was the reason that I'd been driving around. I could tell in the way that he confessed, and it all made sense. I pulled back, the nurse long gone, and looked up into his hazel eyes.

"I wasn't driving around because I was angry."

His brow furrowed and he spoke softly. "What do you mean?"

"I wasn't blowing off steam because I was upset. That wasn't why I got caught in the storm." And then my heart ached because I knew his present was still in the car, and I didn't know if it was even usable now. "I was…" I gasped with my realization. It didn't matter. He would still blame himself. Whether I was out because I was angry at him or out because I had been getting his Christmas present, the point is that I was in that storm because of him, one way or another. Dang, Mason still was going to feel guilty either way.

"What is it?"

"I was coming home from…getting your Christmas present."

His lips fell open and he took a deep breath. "What?"

"It's in the car. That's why I was out. Not because I was angry." I chuckled wryly. "I was trying to surprise you."

I expected his face to fall, his breaths to turn angry, and his fist to clench with hatred for himself. But he half-smiled. "Really? I was so worried when you weren't at your parents'. I thought…I had messed everything up. And then when Adeline called and said she called you, I thought you'd never take me back. I thought I'd never get to clean up all this mess. And then she said that the line went dead and there was so much noise..." He shook his head, his hair a mess on his head. A sexy mess. "I thought I had lost you forever."

"I'm right here," I promised and gripped the nape of his neck tighter.

He pulled my hand up. The left one. "Is there anything else you want to ask me? Anything at all? I promise I'll tell you the truth, the whole truth." He kissed the ring on my finger, his eyes closed.

I shook my head. "No, Mason. I trust you."

He squinted up at me and spoke against my fingers. "Why?"

"Because you came for me." I could taste the fresh tears that fell over my lips. "You saved me. Again."

"Again?" he said confused but adorably hopeful as he leaned toward me.

"You saved me the first time when I opened my eyes and you were there in the hospice, taking care of me, fighting for me, always waiting for me to wake up."

"I had to," he said vehemently against my cheek. "Because you saved me first. At that party when I looked into your sad eyes and saw how much a person can want to change...it not only makes them able to, it makes them worthy of it. For the first time since my mom's accident, you gave me a piece of hope that I could one day be worthy of it, too."

"You are," I insisted and kissed his jaw.

He pressed his lips to my ear. "I love you so much, Em."

When he looked back at me this time, it was a quick glance before closing his eyes and touching his lips to mine. It was bridled and I didn't want that right then. My body was sore and ached in a strange way, but I wanted to feel his passion all over me, crawling through my veins and under my skin. I licked at his lips before pressing closer. "Whoa," he said gently. "Easy, baby." He gave me a stern look. "I just got you back. You need to rest and—"

I was having none of the "rest" talk. I had spent six months of my life resting. I leaned back onto my pillow and took him with me. He groaned, a small protest that carried no real punch, and leaned over me, his palms on either side of me. This time when I opened my mouth to him, he dove head first. Moving my favorite hand up to my face, he held me in place for a series of kisses and licks and bites that had me forgetting me were at a hospital and wanting it to be our honeymoon.

When he pulled back with a small laugh, I scowled. "I wanted to kiss you so badly that day in your room at the hospice on your bed. The day we were supposed to have a date and I was late."

"The day you teased me with your 'I just wanted to taste that coconut' line," I said in my best Mason voice.

He smiled, full-wattage. "Yeah. That."

"Why were you late?"

"Mamma had a doctor's appointment that day and the nurse's son got sick at the last minute, so she couldn't take her."

I frowned and chided softly. "You could have just told me."

"I know." He nodded. "I wish I had. I just loved the way we were and I thought if you found out about me you'd want nothing to do with me."

"But you didn't know that it would make me love you even more for it, did you?"

He smiled bashfully, but right into my eyes. "I should have. I'm sorry I didn't trust you."

"Mason, you got hypothermia for me." Even saying it brought on a fresh round of tears. I smiled through them. "It's all forgotten."

118

He sighed and leaned his forehead to mine. "Tell me you still love me."

"I never stopped," I whispered.

He lifted his head just barely, just enough to see my face. He groaned, "I love you, Em."

"I love you."

He scooted as close as he could and held my face gently. "Thank you for not leaving me here without you."

I felt a sob break free of my lungs as the fact of how close I'd really been to death sank in. The nurse said they had to bring me back…

I didn't want to know right then what exactly that entailed. But soon I'd get Mason to tell me the story.

"Thank you for coming to get me."

His thumbs caressed achingly slow across my cheeks. "I will forever do that." He smiled and glanced out the window. It was bright and white. The storm had calmed, leaving a peaceful, quiet morning behind. Funny how that seemed to be the theme of our lives."Merry Christmas, baby."

Useless Fact Number Eight

Dolly Parton once anonymously entered a Dolly Parton look-alike contest…and lost to a drag queen.

Mason

Emma's parents were relieved, to say the least. They were also very upset with me that I hadn't gotten in touch with them sooner. I didn't tell them the extent of Emma's situation. They thought I went out and found her right away. They didn't know their daughter almost died again. I didn't have the heart to tell them over the phone. They didn't know that I'd stayed in bed with Emma all night to keep her warm and stave off hypothermia, and then long after that because I couldn't make myself leave her. I stood at the desk of the nurse's station, the landline phone to my ear, and wanted to laugh at them the way they handed the phone back and forth, grilling me, laying into me, and then thanking me within seconds of each other.

Emma couldn't go home today, but she was in excellent spirits. It was Christmas after all. Her family was bringing the Christmas to her as soon as the roads were cleared.

And they said they would check on my mom before they came there since my truck got towed from the ambulance bay this morning with a dead battery. But that was OK. It was worth it.

I went back into the room with her and watched her sleep as I waited in my green scrubs. The news had said we were in a state of emergency from the storm, so there were plenty of things still not working properly, cell phones being one of them.

I sat there, waiting and watching until her family showed up. I wondered what Rhett and Isabelle were going to think of my small, normal house. They'd never been there, but they were going to be my in-laws, so they better get used to it.

However, I was shocked when I saw the officer from last night come through the doors and head right for me. He stared at me expectantly and then sighed. "Well? You found her, didn't you? How is she?"

"I found her." I crossed my arms and pushed through Emma's door open for him to follow me. "I thought you said no one would come out on Christmas to check on people?"

"Well," he twisted his mustached lips, "my girls understand that Daddy has to go help people sometimes. They think I'm a superhero for it."

"You came up here just to see if Emma was OK?"

"Yeah." He handed me a cup of coffee I hadn't even seen him holding because I'd been so surprised as he looked at her. "She doing all right?"

I told him everything that happened after I'd left him. He kept whistling and hissing in sympathy. I thanked him for the coffee and he said for us to take it for what it was—a Christmas miracle. He also said he'd look around and find out who the snowplow driver was on that road, find out why he left the scene, and if he got the make and model of the truck who ran Emma off the road. He said it was a long shot. Since the plow hadn't stopped, he probably hadn't seen or heard anything in the cab of that big truck with the piles of snow flying up. I agreed, hating it but accepting that he was going to look into it, and shook his hand before he left.

I gave him Adeline's phone number, but he said the line had been disconnected. He said he didn't think any criminal charges would be brought up on her. She hadn't officially been harassing us. Keeping photos isn't a crime, he said. The texts were annoying, but since the phone had been disconnected, no criminal charges were possible unless she called again from another line. Her apartment was almost empty when they went there. I doubted that we'd ever hear from her again. It looked like she had skipped town, and that was just fine by me.

I knew it wasn't Adeline's fault directly, any of it, but I couldn't help but hold a piece of blame in my gut for her. They were my actions though. I had left my phone that day and I had chosen not to tell Emma about Adeline and the one date we'd had. So, I shouldered that and decided it was way past time to move on.

When I heard Isabella call through the door that they were there, I reached over to rub Emma's cheek. "Wake up, baby."

She did, almost immediately moving her fingers to press the buttons on her bed to sit up. She looked up and smiled. "Mrs. Wright."

I turned, confused, to see my mom in her wheelchair, Emma's dad with his hands on the handles, and the nurse beside them. They had brought my mom for me? He smiled and shrugged over her shoulder. "It's Christmas."

Before I could look back, Isabella was engulfing Emma and then apologizing for squeezing too hard. They brought a couple of presents and hot apple cider. Or what was once hot. Now it was lukewarm, but it didn't matter. We were all together and that was all that *did* matter.

When Emma asked about her brother and sister, her mother said the airports were closed. She was sure they weren't able to fly in, but couldn't get a hold of them. So they wouldn't be there for Christmas, and with the way things looked, maybe not the wedding either. Emma was bummed, I knew, because she felt the need to get to know them, to have them there, being their sister, remembering how to be.

When Isabella pulled a few small gifts from her bag and laid them on Emma's lap, I recognized them immediately. And so did Emma. They were the Christmas presents her parents had brought to the hospice for her the year before, the ones that sat in the window. She refused to open the presents before. She said that her parents had bought those for the "other" Emma and it didn't feel right to open them. But Isabella had gone up into her room and gotten them on purpose.

Emma looked at them and up at Isabella. She shook her head. Isabella touched her hand. "We bought them for you. Old you, new you, doesn't matter. We bought these for our daughter. It's time you see what we gave you, Emmie."

It was the first time they called Emma *Emmie* and she didn't flinch or make a face. I thought she was going to refuse, politely, but she surprised me. She surprised us all by picking up the biggest of the small packages and twisting it in her fingers. She smiled and put her finger under the crease of that pretty paper, but before she pulled it free, she looked up at me.

I leaned back into the door with the force of that gaze. I felt my breath fall in and out as we stared at each other.

I smiled, knowing it was crooked and my adoration for her was right there on my face. She smiled back and ripped the paper before looking down at it. Peeling it open and seeing the small box, she laid the paper down gently. She glanced up at her mother and opened the maroon box to reveal a locket. She lifted it from the satin. It was a silver oval on a long chain. She turned it over and smiled. Her mom sat on the bed beside her and took it from her. She helped her put it on and leaned back, lifting it in her fingers. "Remember my mom's necklace?" She showed her the one around her own neck. "We got you one to match. E. It stands for Emma, Em, Emmie. All of it. It doesn't matter what we call you, what you remember, or who you marry. You are our daughter," she said and smiled, letting the tears fall. Emma pressed her lips together, her own eyes glassy."Always have been, always will be."

They group-hugged with Rhett, so I went and knelt in front of Mom while they talked. "Hey."

"Mason," she said in her usual confusion. I coaxed her into the present and I took her with me to get everyone something hot to drink. In the small vending room we rounded up cups of hot chocolate. Emma was going to have to get used to my love for the hot brew. Mom used to make it for us when we were kids. We'd chop wood on the weekends for the fireplace and then come in and she'd have it ready for us. We'd sit by the fire and get warm by the wood we worked so hard for, back when Milo was still around.

I took a deep breath as we walked back, a tray of cups in my hands. I hadn't heard anything about Milo or from him in a while. Weeks. It had never been this long before and it didn't make me feel better to not have to go save him all the time. It made me worry why I didn't need to. Was he in jail? Did he move away? Something worse?

I pushed all that away and pressed my hip to the door to push it open. I held the door open for Mamma with it and let it close behind us softly. Rhett and Isabella were back to sitting in the chairs on the other side.

I went to give them both a cup and Isabella reached up, taking my face in her hands. Her lip trembled as she pulled me to her. I held the cups off to the side and wondered what in the world was… Ah. I peeked over at Emma and saw her face, adoration spelled plainly across it. She told them about me finding her.

She released me. "We love you, Mason. I'm so glad you were brought to us. Thank you for what you did."

"Yeah, son," Rhett continued and shook my hand. It was like it used to be, back when I was just Emma's therapist, back before she stole my heart and they no longer wanted me to have anything to do with her. Back when they respected me and knew I'd take care of their daughter, no matter what. Finally, after months, I could see that respect back in his eyes. It was surreal because I had been sure I'd never see it again.

"You don't need to thank me." I chuckled. "It was completely selfish. I can't imagine living without her. I just…had to find her."

"And you had to risk your life, huh?" Isabella asked.

I shrugged, rubbing my neck self-consciously. "I had to."

I felt Emma's stare on my face and turned to her. She lifted her hand and beckoned me to her. I started to sit in one of the hideous brown chairs, but she shook her head and tugged me to sit on the bed with her. "Right here," she commanded.

We stared at each other and everyone else fell away. She smiled coyly and toyed with my fingers in her hand as she let me see how happy she was, the long chain and locket hanging from her neck. A yellow scarf and a sparkly headband also lay in her lap.

If I ever wondered if she really loved me before, that thought was obliterated by the absolute love I saw in her eyes as she looked up at me.

I answered her smile and she raised it with a grin. A tired grin because she had been through the wringer, but a grin nonetheless. I cupped her cheek. "You need to rest, sweetheart."

She nodded. "I'm about to fall over. I'm sorry."

"Don't be. You earned it."

I went to move away and she gripped my arm tighter. "Please don't go."

I leaned into her. "Not for the world," I whispered into her ear and then pressed my lips to her forehead while simultaneously pressing the button to make the bed lay flat.

Her dad glanced over at me and back to her, knowing there was something epic going on, but as much as I liked her dad, he'd never understand. Emma and I had saved each other in more ways than one. The way I loved this girl *was epic* and it changed the air around us with its sparks. Shakespeare could write a sonnet just for her and it still wouldn't capture all the things I wanted to say.

"I'll be here when you wake up. Sleep, you."

She smiled, her eyes closing. "Bye, you."

I tucked the blanket up to her chin and around her shoulders and sat at the foot of her bed. I pushed the blanket back a little and began to rub her leg for her as she slept. It was that one thing that I felt like I had control over. This had been my job when she was in a coma; it was my job when she was healing, it was my job when she was running from the old her, and it was my job now, to take care of her always. Our parents were deep in conversation, and I was paying them very little attention. I lifted her leg, kissing the top of her foot, before tucking it under the covers and starting on the other one.

Emma would be making a joke right now about me being a legs man. I chuckled under my breath. That was absolutely true, but this was just one way I knew to show my love for her, to take care of her. It was nothing but an act of service and love, and Emma would have a lifetime of this to look forward to.

Our parents and I talked for a while. Em's parents enjoyed immensely the stories my mother conjured of our past Christmases. When they agreed to take my mom home, they tried to take me with them. I needed a shower, I needed clean clothes, Isabella could stay—they tried it all.

I refused, gladly. I promised Em I would stay and I planned to. I wasn't leaving until she could come with me.

Useless Fact Number Nine

Studies show that 70% of people who marry their best friend stay married their entire lifetime.

Emma

I will not postpone.

I said it a hundred times by the end of that week, at least. Mom was adamant, but I was even more so. I stared out the window at the snow that blanketed the yard. It hadn't stopped all week.

The snow was still knee-high, making the walk in snow-white heels down the sidewalk more than a challenge, but not a deal-breaker.

Because of the weather and the damage all around the county, Mom was worried that most of the guests wouldn't be able to come. She was worried about *that*. She said, *Who has a wedding the week after they get into an accident?* Me, that's who. She would roll her eyes, smooth her silk shirt, take a deep breath, and then go again, moving about the house, getting things to her liking for the wedding.

The church was out. A tree had fallen in the ice storm and smashed a corner of the sanctuary. Mom threw one of her tantrums fit for Scarlett O'Hara herself about that one. I didn't care where we had it. When she saw how adamant I was about the wedding still taking place, she said we'd have it at the house. They put a sign up at the church saying the wedding had been moved here for anyone who missed the message.

And the little tornado that was my mother got to work, freaking over every little detail and having coronaries every time someone called to say they couldn't come or the caterer tried to talk her out of the crazy things she had wanted and still wanted…in the foyer of their large home. "Ma'am, it's not prudent to have an ice sculpture inside the house in the winter when you'll have the heater and fires going."

A knock on the door pulled me to look over my shoulder. My slack-jawed father stared until I turned and shrugged. "So is it safe to come down or has the wrath of Isabella Walker just begun?"

He smirked. "I've got it on good authority that Mason is here. And he's melting your mother's heart as we speak." His smile changed. "It's time. And you look..." He sighed. "You look beautiful, Emma."

I smiled, smoothing my dress. "Thanks, Dad." I looked him right in the eye. "Is this what you imagined I'd look like on my wedding day?"

He smiled, coming and putting his hands on the tops of my arms. "Better. I honestly never thought you'd be this happy."

"Really?" I said, surprised. And a little off-put.

"I thought you were going to marry Andy," he told me wryly and twisted his lips.

"So…not all bad came from the coma?" I said in a small voice.

"Something I've learned is there isn't anything in our life that is for nothing. We aren't just wandering around waiting for time to pass and hoping good things come our way. The things that are handed to us are for a reason." He hugged me to him, placing my head under his chin. "We aren't given more than we can handle." I let that sink in. Mason had said something similar many times. "I thought I'd break in two when we found out about your accident. I thought to myself, how in the world am I going to survive this? But it wasn't me who needed to survive it, it was you. And you're doing a pretty darn good job."

It was futile to try to stop the tears after that. He held me like that for a while, even though he had said it was time to go.

I looked out my window over his shoulder and shivered at the snow that whipped around in the daylight. Sighing, I took my white peep-toe pumps, that mom insisted were some designer I'd always wanted to wear on my wedding day, and slipped my feet into them.

I did the cliché last look as I straightened the veil behind me, glancing toward my strapless dress with a cinched waist. The bandage over the stitches in my head that was covered so nicely with my curled hair that mom had done for me. And it hit me, it did, just like they say it does. I looked at myself, the little diamond earrings that I 'borrowed' from Mom who had worn them on her day, the 'old' platinum bracelet on my wrist that was Grandma's, Mom said the Jimmy Choos we bought constituted as something 'new', and then yesterday morning, when I finally got to come home from the hospital, I found a little bag on my bed with Christmas wrapping. Mason said not to open it until he left that night, so I didn't. When I finally got to, I recognized Mason's scribble on the card.

I never got to give you your other Christmas present. I hope you like it. I'm not being too presumptuous, am I...Mrs. Wright?

I opened that bag to reveal the most delicate yet sinful looking baby blue garter belt, lace trimmed, not overdone. There was a small black satin bow in the front that made it feel even that much more sexy. My breath rattled in excitement and I cursed him through a text about teasing me with *that*.

Now, I couldn't see it in the mirror as I examined myself, but I knew it was there. Mason had gone back to the car the day the wrecker went to tow my car from the wreckage site. He got most of the things out of my car for me the day I was there, and luckily the tattoo gun had survived. When he came back into my room, I was just coming back from a shower. I stood, brushing my hair, hating that I had to stay another night. He was wearing a half-grinning, half-stunned face. "You got me a custom Danny Fowler machine."

"Yeah. Is that a good one?" I asked and winced. Maybe I shouldn't have bought it for him. He knew all about them. "I probably should have just given you a gift card or—"

He was on me before I could finish. His arms wound themselves around me gently and he palmed the small of my back before moving his very warm hands to my behind. He held me against him, supporting me and letting me lean on him. I gasped into his mouth in a way that told him to keep going. It had been days since he had really kissed me. The week before our wedding, no less. I missed him even though he was there every day. I missed him *this* way.

That boy put some serious moves on me in that hospital room.

And now, as I remembered the garter belt on my thigh, I couldn't wait for him to take it off. I looked at myself in that mirror and no longer felt the insecurities and inadequacies that clung to me like before.

This wasn't the life the old me would have picked or even wanted. But I wanted it. I chose it. It chose me. I would forever be grateful for the way life *doesn't* turn out like we planned.

I looked at my father in the mirror and we smiled, knowing it was our cue. I let him lead me to the staircase, seeing all the people down there in my peripheral, knowing Mason was there, but I couldn't look yet. My heart beat hard but slow. I wasn't scared or nervous. I was *really* ready to have his last name be mine and cement myself to my new world. This act, this decision, showing everyone he was mine was taking hold of the new me in a way I hadn't been able to do yet. My heart beat just for him in that moment.

Mom had the huge foyer all decked out with…stuff. Pretty white ribbons were tied around the posts and yellow roses were everywhere. There were no chairs. The people stood on either side, leaving a path for me to go straight to Mason.

I finally lifted my gaze and was assaulted by his smile. Mason was a smirker, a crooked-smile kind of guy. But this…this was full on, showing his teeth and his soul, everything. I gripped Dad's arm harder so I wouldn't trip down the stairs. When we reached the bottom, I let Mason pull me to him like a magnet.

He laughed softly as I grabbed the lapel of his jacket and tugged him a step closer. I heard laughter around me, too. I didn't even know who the guests were because I couldn't take my eyes off my Mason. I whispered in a groan, "Mason."

He leaned close and whispered, his mouth on my ear, "So glad you're as happy to see me as I am you."He took my earlobe, earring and all, into his mouth and sucked before releasing it, but still holding me close as he looked at the preacher in a *Let's get on with it* motion. My knees actually buckled a little.

I was happy he was holding me up at that point. His arm and hand were low on the bodice of the back of my dress. Low enough for me to have difficulties concentrating, but not low enough that my father would want to murder him on the foyer's travertine tiles.

I did as I was told by the preacher, though in honesty, he could have been asking me if I skipped backwards with an alligator skin purse in the light of the harvest moon. Mason held all my attention and I didn't know what I was agreeing to. Even though I wasn't looking at him, my entire being was focused on him. The way he smelled, the warmth that came from the arm around me, the way he kept looking at the side of my face, his sexy, adorable smile still in place.

As long as I got Mason at the end of this thing, it didn't matter what the preacher was saying.

When he finally got to the *kiss your bride* part, I was in a haze. Mason took his time, which made me burn even more for him. He cupped my face with his hands and leaned in. The bandages around his knuckles were still there. I could see them in my peripheral, and I knew the one on his arm was there under his suit, too.

My hero.

My skin tingled with anxiousness. He barely touched my lips with his before grinning. "Coconut," he growled happily before taking my mouth like it was rightfully his.

Because it was.

The claps and *aww*s and whoops behind me didn't stop me. I clung to his jacket, but didn't need to because his arms held me firmly against him, wrapped around my lower back. The small moan that I felt more than heard over the clapping had me smiling against his lips. I only opened my eyes after he pulled back and put his forehead to mine. He said softly, "You ready?"

I nodded. "You can't back out now, Mr. Wright."

His grin grew. "Not a chance."

He took my hand, turning me and proudly holding it in his. I finally got a look at the people in the room. Lots of people I didn't know, or remember at least, stared at us with smiles. It really didn't matter if I remembered them or not. They were happy for us and that was enough for me.

He tugged me with him and we moved through the crowd of people to the back of the room, toward the formal dining room. But I sucked in a breath at the boy standing in the back of the room. I squeezed Mason's hand to get his attention. When his grip tightened noticeably, I knew he'd seen his brother as well.

Milo leaned against the back wall, his hands in his pockets, a pair of boots, clean jeans, and big black coat on. He was still as thin and pale as last time, noticeably strung out, but trying to make the effort. He just looked at us. His face didn't show any emotion as all until Mason started to move that way. Milo stiffened and stood straight. He shook his head like he wanted to say something, but just…couldn't.

I looked up at my husband's face to find him so torn up. I rubbed his arm and watched as Milo stared, his face changing. I knew he was about to leave because the resolve was settling over his features. I got it. He still loved his brother, of course he did, and he wanted to see his brother married and happy. But he wasn't ready to reconcile.

I gave him a small smile to convey that I understood. I mouthed, "Thank you."

He nodded once to me and a ghost of a smile showed up as his gaze switched from me to Mason. Then with his chest rising with a deep breath, he turned to go. I thought Mason might chase after him, but he didn't. And then I wondered if Milo had ruined the reception for me by upsetting Mason, but when I pulled his face to look at me, he looked peaceful.

"He's going to come around one day," he said quietly. "Isn't he?"

I nodded. "You did good taking care of him. He wanted to see you happy."

He smiled. "He saw that for sure." He leaned in to kiss my upturned lips and the claps sounded again. I felt a blush starting to creep up. I'd forgotten everyone could still see us. I wondered if anyone else had seen Milo. I wondered if Milo talked to his mom.

I wondered how long it would be before we saw him again.

Useless Fact Number Ten

Diet Coke destroys tooth enamel as much as meth and crack cocaine.

Mason

I danced with every person in that room but Emma. They were hell bent on getting their dances in. I danced with Isabella and all the ladies who claimed to be this person or that—an aunt, an acquaintance, a family friend.

When I danced with Mamma in her wheelchair, she stayed lucid through it and I was happy. I had learned to grab those moments and make them count instead of spending all my time wishing for things that wouldn't come. She smiled and laughed as we danced to *Fools Rush In*. She sang the words and I felt lighter and lighter, if not more anxious to take my bride away.

When I looked up and found Emma watching us, a hand on her father's arm, I jolted with anxiety at first because she was crying. But when her eyes drifted to Mamma's, I knew there was nothing to be alarmed about. My wife was just being sentimental.

My wife.

And then I had just…had enough. The cake was done, the bouquet had been tossed, and I announced that I was going to dance with my wife and then we were going on our honeymoon.

The garter belt toss did not take place. Number one, there weren't that many single guys there anyway, and number two, I had bought it for her. Me. And I wanted that little blue scrap of material to be for my eyes only.

Just knowing it was there under her dress, like a little secret between her and me, drove me mad ever since I saw her come down the stairs.

I realized I hadn't even had the chance to tell her how beautiful she was yet. So I thanked Mom for the dance and took her back to her table before setting my eyes on the prize and making my way to her. She laughed at something her dad and his colleague said, but I couldn't help myself as I pressed my lips to the back of her neck in a quick swipe before telling them I was stealing her away.

She didn't even look back at them, just let me tow her. When we reached the middle of the dining room floor and had it all to ourselves, I was glad that the lights were down, because I *had* to press her against me, take all of her that I could.

Our temples rested against each other's and my hand on her lower back pressed her hips to mine. I kissed her cheek and asked, "Are you happy?"

She didn't lift her head, but I felt her smile against my cheek. "What kind of question is that?"

"The only one that matters right now."

"I'm so…" she pressed her lips to the skin under my ear, "incredibly happy."

"That's good. That's all I want. You know that, right?"

"That's why I love you so much."

"I'll never get tired of hearing you say that." I did lean back this time, even as our hips swayed, and I looked at her gorgeous eyes. "I haven't had the chance to tell you how beautiful you look yet. But, Em…you are. Beautiful and then some."

"Thanks," she whispered. "So are you."

I smiled. "You mean devilishly handsome."

She smiled back, but it was sincere. "No. I mean…beautiful. But you aren't in seven-hundred dollar heels that are killing your feet."

I felt my eyes bulge. "High heels?" She nodded. I lowered my voice. "Let me see." She obliged me, stopping our dance to lift the bottom of her dress just barely, showing me the ankle-view side of her white, sparkly heels. I groaned a little, thinking about that ankle attached to that leg and those heels. I chuckled against her temple.

She grinned. "You have a little *thing* about legs, don't you?"

"I will forever be a *legs man*."

I couldn't stop caressing her face. My thumb made love to that cheek, and I leaned in close and relished in her every feel, every touch, every sigh. Eventually, I'd had enough. I couldn't stand it another second. I pulled back and it must have been on my face that my limit had been reached. Or maybe she was just as ready as I was. I wanted her alone, all to myself.

We both dressed in our jeans quickly, her in her room and I was in her brother's. She came down the stairs again with everyone cooing and fawning all over the teary mother and the bride as she prepared to leave with her husband.

After putting our boots on and zipping up Emma's big black coat over her yellow v-neck sweater, I took her hand and led her through the doorway into the bright white of the snowy driveway. We said goodbye to our parents and waved to everyone else as they watched us go. A few of the guests were staying at the B&B also, including my friends Rob and Patrice, since they were in no position to drive home to the next town. It was almost dark, but the streetlights and snow made it seem like it was glowing.

We were assaulted by birdseed and cheers. Emma squealed and giggled as I tried to shield her. I tucked her quickly into her side of my truck—my big, rugged truck that was decorated with ribbons and cans. I climbed in and drove the short distance to the B&B. There was no checking in to do. They got our bags that I had packed earlier from the back seat and took them up to the room. I said we had one small errand to run and we'd be back. They looked curious, but said they'd leave the door unlocked for us.

I took Em to the house instead. I went around to her side and pulled her from the high seat into my arms. She didn't ask why we were there or what we were doing. She let me lead her and knew that I had a plan. It was one of the many reasons I loved her—that she trusted me with abandon.

I towed her to the porch and leaned into her smiling face, kissing her lips before lifting her into my arms. She giggled as I pushed the door open and set her feet inside the threshold. "Welcome home, Emma Wright."

She smiled, biting into her lip. "Thank you. And what are we going to do now?"

I pulled her face up with my finger under her chin while hooking my arm around the small of her waist.

"What I've wanted to do for weeks now," I said low. She shivered and her smile showed nervousness, but happiness, too. I felt bad for teasing her…almost. I turned from our embrace, grabbing a sleeping bag and a thick blanket. She raised a curious brow but followed when I ticked my head.

I brushed off most of the snow and laid the sleeping bag down over the picnic table. Then beckoned her to me as I lay down. We snuggled under the blanket, our booted feet touching. She was turned toward me with my arm around her, but could still look up into the dark sky that was only illuminated by the stars.

The same stars that I poured my heart out to Emma under, to anyone, for the very first time. Though I fought it then, I still knew that my life would never be the same.

I wanted to make love to her, of course I did, but as our first act as a married couple, I wanted to go back to the beginning. The start of a real *us* that was tangible and not just wishful thinking and hoping, but a reality that had scared the hell out of me.

"I don't know what the stars' names are," I began and loved how she watched me, so enraptured. "I don't know the constellations or what they mean. I know this— that when I brought you out here that day, I hadn't intended on telling you everything. I figured when I told you what happened that night and how my friend died and my mom…how I thought it was all my fault, that you'd think I was a lost cause. I thought I could piss you off and you'd leave forever."

She shook her head, her lips lifting wistfully. "No, you didn't get rid of me that day."

"Or any day after that." The snow had stopped and I shooed a snowflake from the hair that was rebelling against her skullcap. "I barely heard the preacher today because of everything that has happened this week and all the weeks since I've met you. It consumed my thoughts. I've made so many mistakes and I never developed the ability to let things roll off my back. I'll work on it, I promise."

She nodded. "I know you."

"I promise to always tell you *everything*. And I promise to hang my towel up after a shower."

She seemed to see where this was going. "I promise to ask before jumping to conclusions."

"I promise that I'll put my shoes away and you'll never trip on them coming in the door."

She smiled and a tear escaped the corner of her eye. Anyone would laugh that she was crying over my shoes, but she wasn't. God, I loved her so much right then for *getting* me. For getting us. I loved her for getting the way I needed to lay my heart out there for her so she could see all the wide spaces that were yet to be filled, but would be, even now as she told me the ways she wanted to love me.

"I promise that I won't ever make you choose between your mom and me. I know you're a package deal and I wouldn't have it any other way."

I huffed a sigh and gripped her thigh under the blanket to pull her closer. "I promise that I'll support you, no matter what you choose to do after school."

She wiggled one of her legs between mine, shifting her hips closer. "I promise that I'll understand when you have to leave for Milo, and I know you two will reconcile one day."

I gulped. Seeing Milo tonight had thrown me. One, I didn't know how he even knew about the wedding, and two, why would he come if he hated me? It gave me hope inside my chest that I thought was long gone. "I promise that no matter what happens in this life, I'll always love you. Always."

She closed her eyes, sniffling, and smiled. "I promise I won't park behind you in the driveway so you can't get out."

"I'll always call if I'm going to be late."

"I won't forget the hot chocolate from the grocery store."

I grinned and tightened my grip on her. "I'll tell you how much I love you every…single…" I kissed the tip of her freezing cold nose. "Day."

"I'll only ever let you tattoo me."

My chest rumbled at that and I growled something along the lines of, *That's right you will*. "I'll rub your calf muscles anytime you need me to."

"I promise I won't tell anyone how ticklish you are."

I smirked. "I'll always remember what an empty theater and a *Bonanza* marathon does to you."

"I also won't spill the beans that you're a closet guitarist."

"Hardly." I smiled. "I promise to help you fill your list with everything you've ever wanted to do."

She put her gloved palm on my cheek. "I'll never regret…anything. Ever."

"I'll never lie to you."

"I'll never leave angry."

"I won't ever take you for granted."

"I won't…" She did the smile-cry again. "I won't ever forget. You or this or us." She took a deep breath as I felt those words punch into my guts. "I won't ever forget you," she said again, softer.

That was it, the breaking point. I leaned up and over her and kissed her softly. We'd never really talked about it before, but several other people have asked what I would do if Emma remembered everything. I always told them that it wasn't likely, but if it did happen…I didn't know how she would process it all.

With her arms wrapped around my neck, she reiterated. "I mean it. I'll never forget you. Even if my memories came back," she shook her head violently looking up at me, "I'd still remember you and love you. That won't ever go away."

"Even if it did, I wouldn't let you go without a fight," I told her and hovered there, just out of reach of her lips.

She smiled and pulled her fingers through my belt loops. "Promise?"

"Hell yeah, baby. I love you," I groaned those words into the skin of her neck.

"I love you. I'm so glad you wanted to marry me even though I'm unfixable," she said breathlessly.

I shook my head. "You made loving you so easy."

I kissed her mouth over and over again. It was so quiet out there, our noises sounded so loud and erotic. I leaned back a little on my elbows to gain some control. "You're not upset about not getting the big fancy church wedding, are you? The doves? The ice sculpture?"

"I don't care about any of that. I just wanted you."

I chuckled. "Wow. You are feeding my ego like a prisoner's last meal."

She bit her lip, the corner of her mouth lifting. "It's true." She looked up at the stars and then back down to me with a strange look. "Can I ask you something?"

I knew what was coming. "You wanna know why I brought you here instead of straight to the B&B to ravage you in our room."

She huffed a small laugh and nodded. "Yeah. Not that I'm not happy right now. I love that you brought me here, to this spot. It's so ridiculously sweet of you. I was just…curious."

I licked my lip before speaking. "I want you so bad." I could hear her breaths."I've wanted you for months and you've made it very…difficult." She just smiled at that. "But this spot right here, on this picnic table, where I brought you to spill my guts? I used to lie out here at night. It felt like the only place in the world that I was the same person I used to be. I brought you here because more than wanting to make love to you, I wanted to *show* you how much I loved you first."

"I love this spot," she said. "Thank you." I smiled and nodded once, knowing over the years that we would spend hours and hours out there. "So you want me?" she breathed.

"You know I do," I said, pressing against her from toe to chest. "And now that you see how much I love you and how happy I am to have you here with me…are you ready to go?"

She nodded, biting her lip again. I quirked a brow. "Nervous?"She nodded again. "Why, baby?"

"It's a good nervous, not bad. I know I'm not a virgin or anything, but I still feel like one. Mainly, I just want to," she took a deep breath, "do things right."

I felt the breath slam in my throat. "Are you serious?" I whispered.

She nodded and squinted her eyes. "Yes."

She thought I was making fun, I realized. I smoothed her cheek with my gloved finger. "Em, I don't think…there's anything you can do that won't be the right thing. Don't you see how crazy you make me when you just look at me? All you have to do is touch me and I'm *gone*."

She eyed my face for a few moments. Then, her lips parted and she leaned up taking my bottom lip into her mouth and sucked.

I groaned loudly, my eyes rolling. "Em, do you really think you don't completely own me?" Her leg hooked over my hip. I groaned again as her hips rolled under mine.

She pressed her lips to my cheek and said in the sexiest, huskiest, most gulp-inducing voice I'd ever heard from that mouth, "I'm ready to go, Mason."

I kissed her with a slow burning passion that surprised even me. My insides quivered with the force of it. But instead, I found myself worshipping her mouth, adoring her lips and tongue, the way they sought my own with such enthusiasm.

I savored her every moan, noise, gasp and flick of her tongue. I could have taken her right there on the picnic table in my backyard under the stars, but when we heard a door shut, I knew the nurse had brought my mom home.

And I was only interested in my wife tonight.

So I helped my giggling wife as we crawled down from the table, sprinted across the yard, and around the side of the house by my old shop to the truck. The drive was short, but felt like forever as she kissed my neck and ran her hand up my leg. I did my own gasping, kissing her as much as I could while still driving in the lines. She hung onto my neck as I rubbed my hand down her leg and back up to the inside of her thigh.

When we pulled into the B&B, I slammed on the brakes sideways in the parking lot, taking up way more than one spot. We practically ran upstairs and I was surprised when we bumped into Rob and Patrice in the hall.

"You're just now getting here?" Rob asked like he couldn't believe it. "Where have you been?"

"We had…an errand to run," I told him as we maneuvered around them.

"Uh." He chuckled like he didn't understand at all. "OK. Well, I was thinking that we could meet up for breakfast or—"

"Rob, shut up," Patrice insisted and looked back at us apologetically. I grinned my gratefulness. "Sorry. We're sure you'd like to *be alone now.*" She glared over at him, hoping he'd get the message.

"We do. Night!" I called over my shoulder and towed Em into the room with me. Rob was asking her what the problem was when I shut the door and locked it.

Without another word, I pushed my wife gently to the door. She was already unbuttoning her jacket and I helped her as I kissed her. Then my jacket was next. She reached on her tiptoes as she kissed me and yanked my jacket down my arms. The next thing to go was our boots. I kicked off mine and then knelt down to take off hers. I let my hands travel her jeaned legs all the way up to her hips as I stood.

When she reached for the hem of my shirt, I let her do it without my help, just lifting my arms and then pressing her there again. I watched her face as I pulled her shirt up slowly over her head. Her eyes never left mine

158

except when the fabric passed over her face. She licked her lips before wrapping her hand around the back of my neck and tugging me down to her.

I lifted her easily, my hands under her thighs, and pressed her to the door gently. I was in no hurry. As long as I had her in my arms, we had this room for an entire four days. I wanted to savor every second of it and make her absolutely never want to leave this room again.

After a long time—minutes, hours, could have been days—I let her down to remove the rest of the barriers of clothing, the final pieces that would make us one. I pressed her arms above her head and whispered for her to stay just like that. She obeyed as I unbuttoned her jeans, kneeling down in front of her to tug them down. I felt my swift intake of breath at what I found. On her thigh, sitting right where it had been all night taunting me, was the blue garter belt I bought for her. The growl that reverberated through me couldn't be stopped. I let my eyes lift to hers and she was wearing a little sideways smile that said she was enjoying my reaction. I finished pulling her jeans off, one leg and then the other. My eyes only left hers when I leaned in to run my fingers underneath the band of that garter. She shivered and shivered again when I kissed the place where the garter met her skin.

I stood and the rest of our clothes dissolved by my nimble fingers, everything except that garter belt. That was staying on. We searched each other with our eyes and the tips of our fingers.

When I carried her to the bed, that we didn't even know the color of, she didn't hold back. And true to my word, I was *gone*.

Useless Fact Number Eleven

To remain in love for a lifetime : listen actively to your partner, ask questions, give answers, appreciate, stay attractive, include your partner, give him/her privacy, be honest and trustworthy, tell your mate what you need, accept his/her shortcomings as who they are, give respect in all things, never threaten to leave, say 'no' to adultery, and cultivate variety in your activities to keep things fresh. You can never say 'I love you' too many times and you should say it every day. Even though you've been together forever it seems, you should still continue to 'date' your mate and find new ways to fall in love with them every. Single. Day.

Emma

A slow burning passion was what I got that first time. It was just as important, if not more so, than an unbridled one. They each have a purpose and each have a way of changing you forever.

And I was changed.

The next time and the time after that was more of the unbridled variety, and then he went back to slow burning. I was glad for the four days we had in that room. I was elated that I never knew what he was going to do next. I decided it was a gift that I couldn't remember all those times with Andy that I read about in my diary, because this what how it was supposed to be. I wasn't thinking about anything else, any other times, the way things might feel different. No. It was just Mason.

We finally came down for breakfast the next day, but it was officially lunch. I couldn't look anyone in the eye. It was hilarious. They knew what we had been doing all night and all morning. It was so weird! Mason laughed at me and didn't hide his smug smile a bit as we ate the eggs and sausage they warmed up for us. He would lean over and kiss me for no reason and then go back to his plate. Then out of nowhere, he would lean in and kiss me again, longer, harder this time, before sitting up straight. He paid no attention to anything going on around us—just me and the food on his plate he needed to replenish his strength.

I closed my eyes and barely suppressed my groan thinking about how amazing Mason had been with me. He seemed to know exactly what I wanted. When I wanted slow, he went slow. When I wanted more…he gave me more. I learned every tattoo on his body and there were a lot. He had one on his lower stomach of a crow that I had never even seen before. He said it was his very first tattoo. He thought it was 'cool' and didn't even know the meaning behind it or anything before having someone slap it on him. Now he loved it, because it was what got him into wanting to do tattoos in the first place.

And the *Em* over his heart? I kissed that ink over and over again, absolutely dying with the way his arms flexed and the muscles moved against my skin as they held me close.

In between those times, he would pull me to lay on his chest and we talked as he played with my fingers in the dark room. We talked about everything. He told me stories about his mom when they were younger. Stories about the stupid things he and his friends used to do, stories about him and Milo when they were kids. I knew he was thinking about Milo coming to the wedding like that. I wondered if he had come to the same conclusion I had about how Milo knew about it. I felt a twinge of regret that I didn't have any stories that I could remember to tell. He just kissed me and shook his head, telling me we'd make new ones together. We only wound up sleeping about five hours all together, but that was more than OK.

When Patrice and Rob came downstairs with their bags in their hands, Mason just tipped his head to them, took my hand, and towed me back upstairs, unwilling to add anyone to our honeymoon. I giggled at him and heard Rob laughing behind us.

After a while of napping and delivered pizza while we watched a Christmas movie, among other things, it was dark when we decided to come back down again. We changed into our swimming suits and though the tub in our room was nice, very nice, we decided to put the amenities of this place to use.

It felt weird to get in a Jacuzzi when there was snow outside, but the back deck was glassed in, a pretty sun porch with flowers and plants everywhere. The ceiling had soft white Christmas-like lights. It was completely perfect and I wondered if the place in the mountains would have been like this.

It felt right to be there.

Mason got in, tossing his towel over the back of the chair before leaning back against the side. The *Em* tattoo sat just above the water. I took off my robe, enjoying the way his eyes followed my every move. I had packed one of the skimpy little red things the old me called a bathing suit for the honeymoon.

I stepped in and he held his hand out to help me in. I settled right onto his lap, his arms snaking around my waist.

"Nice suit," he practically growled.

I laughed and stage whispered close to his mouth, "You've seen me naked. Why do you like it so much?"

"Because…it's hot," he replied against my throat.

"That explains it," I joked. "Same reason why guys like lingerie so much?"

He did a half-gasp, half-sigh thing. "Just you saying that word is so hot, let alone wearing it." He leaned back, his head resting on my arms around his neck. "Which I will not object to."

I giggled, but he reached up to cup my face, his own face thoughtful. "I hope I can make you happy. I won't ever stop trying."

I nodded. "I know that."

"I don't feel like there's all these wide spaces anymore." He lifted my hand from the water, kissed my fingers, and laid our laced fingers over my name on his heart. "I think they're all full up."

I smiled, but knew that was a lie. His brother had an empty space in there. I knew it would all come to a head soon, and I couldn't wait for my Mason to be whole again.

I'd never seen him whole, and I could bet it was a beautiful thing.

"They will be," I promised him. "I know it."

His face showed that he understood my meaning, but he decided not to respond to that. Instead, he said, "Yeah. They'll be filled with little blonde girls who look an awful like you running around our Christmas tree."

That made me smile so big. "And have hazel eyes…like you and be total Daddy's girls."

His smile was gorgeous. He pulled me to him and kissed my mouth reverently. "I will always adore you for seeing the good in me when I couldn't."

My breath caught and held in my throat. "Then we're even."

The End

Be on the lookout for

Wide Open

Milo's story - the third and final book in the Wide Awake
series to release December 2013.

Playlist

(Theme) Waiting for You : Royal Teeth
Below My Feet : Mumford & Sons
Ways to Go : Grouplove
Demons : Imagine Dragons
Wait : M83
Opposite : Biffy Clyro
Whistle for the Choir : The Fratellis
Saved : The Spill Canvas
To Chicago : The Spill Canvas
Ghosts That We Knew : Mumford & Sons
Capital Cities : Safe and Sound
Turn Me On : The Fray
In Silence : New Holland
Beneath Your Beautiful : Labrinth
Midnight City : M83
Serial Sleepers - (Acoustic) : House of Heroes
I Choose You : Andy Grammer

Wide Spaces

is proud to be part of

http://www.newadult12.com/

Shelly is a *New York Times* & *USA Today* bestselling author from a small town in Georgia and loves everything about the south. She is wife to a fantastical husband and stay at home mom to two boisterous and mischievous boys who keep her on her toes. They currently reside in scorching North Florida. She loves to spend time with her family, binge on candy corn, go out to eat at new restaurants, buy paperbacks at little bookstores, sightsee in the new areas they travel to, listen to music everywhere and also LOVES to read.

Her own books happen by accident and she revels in the writing and imagination process. She doesn't go anywhere without her notepad for fear of an idea creeping up and not being able to write it down immediately, even in the middle of the night, when her best ideas are born.

Shelly's website:

www.shellycrane.blogspot.com

Now, please turn the page to enjoy an exclusive
excerpt of the new book in the
Significance series
that will release in 2014,

Undeniably Chosen

One

Ava

I waited for that day, for that one thing to complete me. To feel someone's heartbeat inside my chest and know that it was reciprocated. To find the one who belonged to me and could be the one to make me whole.

I still waited. I was a sophomore in high school. Graduating and heading off to U of T in a just two years so I could be an architect, just like Grandpa.

We just got back from the last reunification. Mom had taken fire for her new rule about the Visionary being able to work and have a day job rather than just…being the Visionary. They wanted her to be 'accessible' at all times and she warred on that she could be accessible and still work with Daddy at the centers as well. That's what cell phones were for.

So I watched as Dad was being extra nice and attentive by cooking dinner that night since, even though she was the Visionary, it sucked when people were against you and questioned your dedication.

Wanna know what else sucked? Being the Visionary's daughter. And the clan leader's daughter deducted even more points.

I loved my parents, don't get me wrong. They were great. Rodney and I both were pretty grounded. We went to the private school here and he played football while I played volleyball. I'd been working at the learning centers for Daddy for a year now.

I loved it, but planned to go work for Grandpa as soon as I graduated from college. Dad was fine with it. He of all people knew what it was like to want to be something, to have the fire for something.

I was fascinated by the thought that I could create something like that.

We used to travel around with Daddy's job, staying in a place for a couple months before moving on to the next place. It might not sound so appealing, but it really was amazing to live in all those states. We lived in New York, Washington, Chicago, Texas, and about fifteen other states. But, when I was almost in high school, they wanted us to settle down, so we moved back to Tennessee and Daddy bought Mom a big, beautiful red house with a wraparound white porch. Rodney's old fort made from wood slats was still in the backyard, though he hadn't been back there in years.

It was our home and I loved it, but also couldn't wait to leave it. My teenage heart was so fickle. But the one thing it wasn't fickle on was wanting my significant.

So, back to the part where I was waiting. Even though I wasn't of age yet, every reunification brought anxiousness for me. I was fifteen. Mom was only seventeen when she imprinted and since all the rules were being broken, I couldn't help but hope that I would imprint soon.

It was more than just wanting to have somebody, it was like this thing in my body was pulled just a little too tight. Just enough to annoy and bother me, but not enough to be painful. My significant was the only one who could make me feel normal. I knew it.

Dad tossed the noodles with the white sauce, Mom's favorite, and divided it onto four plates as our new puppy Mavis rubbed against my leg. Dad glanced up at me with a smile. "Put ice in some glasses for me, sweetheart?"

"Sure."

"Rodney. Rodney!" he called louder.

Rodney took his earphones out and looked at him. "Yeah?"

"Silverware."

"Why are you cooking again?" he asked. "Mom's a way better cook than you."

"Hey!" Dad laughed and slung a noodle at him. It landed on Rodney's face and hair.

He jumped back like that would save him, but it was too late. "Dude!" he shrieked, his voice cracking with puberty as he swatted at his shagged hair. "Dude, my hair!"

Dad and I were laughing so hard, we could barely stand up as Rodney went on. Rodney jumped across the counter and stuck his finger in the sauce before holding it out to Dad. "You're gonna get it, old man."

I ducked out of the way, fearful of my own hair, and giggled by the fridge as they fought and wrestled. I felt Mom's hands on my arms and heard her laugh behind me. "Oh, my. Ava, what's going on?"

"Dad pulled the unforgiveable. He got noodles in Rod's hair."

She giggled and came around me with her blue silk robe on and bare feet. "Is all this for me?" she crooned sweetly, looking around at the mess on the counter.

"Mom, totally his fault." Rodney pointed at Dad shamelessly as he laughed.

"Oh, I believe you." She wrapped her arms around Dad's neck and wiped a smidge of sauce from his cheek with her thumb.

"You believe him over me?" Daddy asked, his voice changing like it always did where Mom was concerned.

She laughed, reaching up on her tiptoes and kissed him. "Thank you for cooking dinner. You didn't have to."

"I wanted to," he replied. His voice and eyes held a reverence that I'd always seen and heard about my whole life, but never experienced. "You earned it. You're such a good woman, and I know the reunifications take it out of you."

I had watched my parents for what seemed like centuries. The way they existed so effortlessly in each other's world and space. They could go minutes without looking away from each other. They kissed constantly. They hugged all the time, stole touches and wrapped their fingers around the other's wrist. I knew it was to feel their calm, to be wrapped in the little bit of bliss that their touch provided.

I felt like I was watching a romance novel play out before my eyes.

"I'm OK," she told him and whispered her next words. "Thank you for this. And for earlier. I really needed it."

"Eew. Gross. Stop," Rodney said, hands up. He threw some forks haphazardly on the table. "Don't you see the way my ears are singed?"

Mom laughed. "I was talking about the bubble bath your father made me, you goober." She reached up again, kissing Daddy on the lips, but he reached around her and drew her in even more. I turned to fill the glasses. It was disgusting, they were my parents after all, but I was also envious. Things were still a little up in the air with the imprints and everything. It seemed that things had gone back to normal for the most part, except there were no more age limits. You met them when you met them and that was that.

So instead of knowing I'd meet the person I wanted most in a few years while in college, I was forced to spend my days *waiting.*

The only thing a girl in high school, who's never dated anyone before, wants is to find someone to love her. I was breaking out and going my own way, and while I was reinventing myself to become the me I would always be, I was dying to throw my epic love story in the mix.

"I love you, Maggie," I heard behind me.

"I love you more."

"Go sit. I'll bring you a plate."

And I waited for it…

The sound of Daddy's palm lightly smacking Mom's butt was my cue that it was OK to turn around now. Mom shook her head at Dad as she took a seat. Dad, smug as all get out, brought her plate, kissing her forehead as he sat it in front of her, before setting the rest of the table and playfully yelling at Rodney to sit down and behave like a Jacobson.

They were so predictable. And adorable. And so in love with each other it hurt to look at them.

Two

Six Years Later
Ava

I yawned and got the stink eye from Professor Gracco. I loved and hated class, but it was the last week of them before summer break. Every class was a yawn-fest. The teachers knew it, but I think it just made them that much more ornery.

The minutes crawled by and my watch kept winking at me, taunting, begging me to keep looking at it so the time would move even slower.

Only two more years of this and I'd graduate and could go work at the firm with Grandpa. Well, not for very long because he was retiring in a few years. But the chance to work with him at all would be worth it. He was happy that I'd decided to come work with them. A few other family members had taken a cue from Dad and went their own way, running a business that they wanted instead.

But they always seemed to be good businesses. Our kind had a knack for smart ventures and risks that paid off. Businesses that were good for more than just us. Like Daddy with his learning centers and my second cousin, who has a horse farm, who started an equestrian riding school.

When the professor took the little golden bell from his desk and jiggled it in the air at us like it was a catholic school and not a college, we knew the class was over. I packed up my things hurriedly and rushed across campus to the coffee shop. Every Friday I brought the whole staff at the center whatever poison that was their favorite beverage.

I was running late. Professor Hubris back there thought that he held our literal futures in his sweaty little hands and it was his duty to teach more than what was lined out in the syllabus.

Like maybe, how to make someone late for work? It didn't matter that my dad owned the company. That actually made me want to be on time even more, so no one could say that I was just there because my father let me be. I wanted to be a good worker, have ethics and values that people could see on me like a Girl Scout badge.

I wanted to earn what I had, not have things handed to me.

So when I ran into the shop and saw Paul at the counter with a carton of coffee cups, I mouthed a 'Thank you' to him. I got the same exact thing every Friday. One white hot chocolate, one black, one vanilla cappuccino with cream and sugar, and for me, a salted caramel iced coffee. There was a long line today, so I waited in it, pulling out my cell to check messages quickly.

A napkin floated to the floor beside me and I reached absentmindedly to pick it up when someone was next to me doing the same thing. Our fingers almost touched on the napkin and my eyes lifted to see dark ones meeting mine. I felt my lips part, not just at his closeness, but at the sheer force of that gaze.

His hair was black and spiked up in the middle in a small faux-hawk. He was tan with a red t-shirt that hugged his neck.

"Thanks," he muttered, his voice as low as gravel. I had to admit that it made me smile for no other reason than the fact that he hadn't taken his eyes off mine yet. He finally, slowly stood.

"No problem," I replied and cleared my throat a little because my voice sounded entirely too affected.

I didn't know what else to say and he just stared, his eyes wandering around my face, before he finally smiled with just one side of his mouth and chuckled a little. "Sorry…you're just really…" He shook his head and stepped back. "Never mind. You go to school here?"

"Yeah. You?"

"Nah," he said, noncommittally. "Just getting some coffee. It was pretty good timing, I guess."

"What was?" I asked, shouldering my bag, refusing to let him go until it was no longer polite to keep him talking.

"Coming here at the same time as you." His smile spoke volumes of things he was thinking that I wasn't privy to. It reminded me of a romance novel…of my parents. I felt a stutter in my chest at what that could mean. "I'm usually here a lot later, but I was early today."

"You're early and I'm late," I said, chagrined that I had forgotten my purpose so easily. I looked over to the counter to see Paul staring an irritated yet intrigued look at my back. I knew he had a little crush on me, but there was no point in pursuing that.

I turned back to dark eyes. He whispered like it was a curse, "Am I keeping you? Do you need to go?"

I stepped off the plank, one hopeful foot in front of the other. "Do you feel that?"

He frowned with his brows, but smiled. "Feel what exactly?"

My spirits fell as fast as they had risen. This was just some college boy checking out girls in the coffee shop. He wasn't Virtuoso, he wasn't a human so intrigued by what was happening to him to press further, and he wasn't someone…that I could go any further with.

I smiled as much as I could, but stepped back. "I really do have to go. I'm really late."

His smile fell and he took a step closer. "Uh…can you stay for one cup of coffee? I'm buying." He tried for a smile again, but I just couldn't let this go any farther.

"I'm late for work already." I turned to give Paul a twenty and told him to keep the change. When I turned back, I expected dark eyes to be gone, done with me, but he wasn't. I smiled and started to move around him toward the side back door.

He called for me to wait a second as he ran back to get his bag from the table, but I kept going. Before I reached the door, his hand gently caught my long sleeve in his fingers. I looked down at his hand first and then at his face. "I'm sorry," he said sincerely. "I'm not trying to be creepy, I just…" He licked his lips.

His red shirt had a fireman symbol on the front with the number 22 in the middle of it. His jeans were dark, worn, and ripped a little at the knee. He wore black boots and had a brown leather band around his wrist that had the word VIVERE on it.

Wow, this boy was going to be a problem if I didn't get away.

"I know. I wish I had time to talk, I really do, but I have to go."

"I do feel it," he said in a harsh voice. "I said I didn't feel it before, but I do."

Every movement but breathing stopped. "Feel what?"

"Like…" He moved his hand to my face and I froze in hopeful awe. He swept my hair back behind my ear. "Like we were meant to be here at the same time."

It was when his finger touched the rim of my ear that I felt my life changing before my eyes. He sucked in a huge breath right along with me and immediately I felt his hands on both sides of my face, pulling me in to press his forehead to mine as we watched the scenes play out. I worried about him. He must be a human because I'd never seen him before and was probably freaking out, but all I could do in that second was cling to his shirt with my empty hand, fisting the fabric and hanging on as I watched our future life together.

In one vision, we were lying in the tall grass somewhere. He ran his fingers up and down my arm. I talked and he listened like his life depended on it. The next one was us as we walked hand in hand down the sand at the beach house my parents owned. He had a bandage across his neck and his arm was in a sling, but he smiled so wide as he looked down at me, black eye and all. And then the third came, us in front of a big house. It was a place that looked familiar, but we stood there, older in our years, proud...like we belonged there on the big lawn and grand landscapes that seemed overgrown, but once beautiful. He was kissing my lips so softly.

We eased out of our reverie and his smile wasn't one of a human, it was one of someone who knew exactly what was going on. He moved us gently, pressing my back to the wall by the back door, but kept my face blissfully captive in his warm hands that I just knew were big and hard-worked calloused. "Oh, my g... It can't be," he said, but his smile refuted those words. "It's...really you."

"And I don't even know your name," I whispered in return.

He chuckled a little, deep and heady. "Seth."

"I'm Ava," I answered before he could ask.

"Ava," he repeated and I felt shivers run over me. He smiled, moving a little closer before letting his forehead touch mine once more. "I can't believe this is happening."

"I don't have to wait anymore," I realized. Even with school and work and everything going on, I was constantly waiting for this. It consumed a little piece in the back of my brain and I was subconsciously always looking for the one whose touch would bind me to him and also set me free.

His smile faltered a little as he leaned his head back. "So…you're Virtuoso."

I nodded. "How come I've never seen you before?"

"We don't…go to the reunifications," he muttered softly. He looked so nervous and I felt the need to comfort him wash over me.

I still held the carton of coffee in one hand so I un-fisted his shirt and reached for his face. I was utterly shocked at how easily it came to me to be with him already. "Hey. What's the matter?"

"I just…" He shook his head and gulped, covering my hand with his on his cheek, like he wanted to keep it there forever. "I don't want to hurt you. I don't want… Gah, I'm so sorry, Ava."

"For what?" I said, but I saw in his mind for the first time. He was thinking about that house from my last vision. I realized that I remembered it from our histories. Our family taught about that…house…

The coffee cups fell from my hand. It was then the world came back to me and I saw several of the people in the coffee shop staring at us. Even Paul had stopped making coffee and was looking at us, like maybe he wanted to intervene.

I pushed Seth's chest a tiny bit, my hands aching and scolding me for doing so. He went without a fight. "Ava," he reasoned, pleaded.

"I've got to go." I turned to go, my heart banging in my chest.

He grabbed my hand gently, his calm, the very thing I'd always wanted, shot through me and I couldn't stop the sigh, yet I still yanked my hand away. "Ava, please. Let's just talk for a minute."

I burst through the door and ran to my Volvo parked in front. Seth followed me, but didn't try to stop me. I got in and shut the door, pressing the push-start button to crank the car. He stood outside my window, gripping his hair in his hands as he watched me back out. I heard him in my head as I peeled from the lot.

I'll wait for you however long you need. It's OK. I understand. I'd hate me, too.

I went straight to the center, blowing through the doors, tears running down my face. Everyone stopped what they were doing and stared, but I looked for Daddy. When I didn't see him with any of the kids, I went right to his office. He was on the phone, but hung up on whoever was on the phone as soon as he saw me.

"Ava-"

"Daddy," I sobbed.

He stood quickly. "What happened?"

"I … imprinted…"

"You did?" He grinned and hugged me to him. "That's amazing, Ava. Where? Who? Why are you crying? Was it-"

"No, Daddy, no." I leaned back.

"What's the matter, baby?" he soothed and smoothed my hair like he had done for my entire life. Always comforting, always willing to bust heads if need be to make me happy. But Dad couldn't fix this.

"Daddy, I imprinted…with a Watson."

Undeniably Chosen

a Significance series novel
Coming Fall, 2014

Made in the USA
San Bernardino, CA
09 May 2014